D0426072

THE (totally not) **GUARANTEED**
GUIDE to STRESSING,
OBSESSING & SECOND-GUESSING

Jessica Darling's ★IT★ LIST 3

THE (totally not) GUARANTEED GUIDE to STRESSING, OBSESSING & SECOND-GUESSING

A NOVEL BY MEGAN MCCAFFERTY

poppy

LITTLE, BROWN AND COMPANY
New York   Boston

Poppy

Hachette Book Group
1290 Avenue of the Americas, New York, NY 10104
Visit us at lb-kids.com

Poppy is an imprint of Little, Brown and Company.
The Poppy name and logo are trademarks of Hachette Book Group, Inc.

The publisher is not responsible for websites (or their content) that are not owned by the publisher.

First Edition: June 2015

Library of Congress Cataloging-in-Publication Data

McCafferty, Megan.
The (totally not) guaranteed guide to stressing, obsessing & second-guessing : a novel / by Megan McCafferty. — First edition.
pages cm. — (Jessica Darling's it list ; 3)
"Poppy."
Summary: "Smarties and skaters unite, collecting signatures on a petition to bring back the school's annual dance. Meanwhile, Jessica faces the outcome of the mortifying-but-true Top Secret Pineville Junior High Crushability Test. Will the dramarama of seventh grade be Jessica's downfall? Not if she can help it"— Provided by publisher.
ISBN 978-0-316-33324-5 (hc : alk. paper) — ISBN 978-0-316-33325-2 (ebook)
[1. Junior high schools—Fiction. 2. Schools—Fiction. 3. Popularity—Fiction. 4. Dating (Social customs)—Fiction. 5. Dance parties—Fiction. 6. Puberty—Fiction.] I. Title.
PZ7.M47833742Tr 2015
[Fic]—dc23

2014033525

10 9 8 7 6 5 4 3 2 1

RRD-C

Printed in the United States of America

*For my friends at HiTOPS adolescent health
services and education center
in Princeton, NJ*

Chapter One

I know I'm not an early bloomer. But am I doomed to be a late bloomer? Or will I bloom sometime in between?

That's what I'm about to find out. Maybe. If I don't get too ACKED out.

I've never given much thought to my body. When I'm hungry, I eat. When I'm tired, I sleep. When I'm sick, I barf. That's the thing about bodies. When you're healthy and everything is functioning properly, your body is pretty easy to ignore. I mean, my body has been with me my entire life, and yet it barely crossed my mind because it just, you know, did the stuff bodies are supposed to do. My body makes me an excellent cross-country runner but a terrible gymnast. My body cannot execute a perfect aerial cartwheel but recovers quickly when an attempt to do so results in an epic face-smash in front of a gym full of bendy, twisty, perky CHEER TEAM!!! wannabes.

You know. For example.

I can't say for sure when my body changed things up. It started doing new stuff. Hard-to-ignore stuff. Like zits.

And my friends' bodies were also changing in noticeable—but different—ways. Like, on the last day of summer before the start of seventh grade, my (old?) best friend Bridget's body ALL OF A SUDDEN transformed from an ordinary sort of body into an extraordinary sort of body that got EVERYONE'S attention on the first day of school. Especially the boys'. Sometimes the changes are less obvious, like when I thought my (new?) best friend Hope was acting all cranky and crampy at a sleepover because she had a nasty stomach virus. She later revealed it was... well, not a virus at all. When she told me her first period was to blame for her bummerific crash on my couch, I was like, DUH.

As an A plus student, I should've known better. Actually, I *did* know better, and I have the perfect test scores to prove it! Last year, our sixth-grade teachers separated the girls from the boys and made us sit in different classrooms to watch The Movie. You know The Movie I'm talking about. It's The Movie about all the stuff that will happen to our bodies as we get older. Calling it THE Movie isn't entirely accurate, because there are actually two versions of The Movie. The girls watched The Movie all about girl stuff, and the boys watched The Movie all about boy stuff, which only *sort of* made sense to me. I mean, wouldn't it be beneficial for there to be just one Movie that covers girl stuff and boy stuff that we all watch together? So girls know what's really going on with boys? And vice versa? Maybe the boy version of The Movie unlocks the biggest mysteries about their behavior. If I had seen it, I might finally, finally, *finally* understand the unique male mind-body chemistry that makes all boys think farts are hilarious. But I didn't see it, so the best I can do is roll my eyes and pinch my nose every afternoon in Woodshop (THE CLASS I'M NOT SUPPOSED TO BE IN), where the boys outnumber the girls eleven (all of them) to one (me).

Rumor has it everyone watches an all-in-one version of The Movie next year in eighth grade. Until then, I guess I'm grateful that our teachers kept us apart. The girl version of The Movie was majorly cringe-worthy (*pee-yoo-ber-tee! men-stroo-ay-shun!*), and I still don't know if I'm capable of watching any version of The Movie in front of *actual boys*, because despite my stellar test scores and full schedule of Gifted & Talented classes, I am surprisingly childish about such things.

Or maybe it's more accurate to say UNsurprisingly

childish. My body isn't any closer to teenagerdom, so why should my brain be any different? Or my heart?

And that's why I'm afraid there's maybe something wrong with me. My body isn't responding the way a seventh-grade girl's body should. And I'm not just talking about the obvious physical stuff, like how I've gotten taller but the overall shape of my body has remained otherwise unchanged since first grade. Or how I'm the only one at my lunch table who hasn't gotten her period. I'm talking about, you know, the kind of boy/girl stuff that The Movie doesn't cover.

What kind of stuff? Here's an example:

Say there's a seventh-grade boy. He's smart. He's a football player. He's considered cute by the girls who consider such things. Boy has girlfriend. He wants to break up with her but can't because his girlfriend had a near-death experience at a sleepover—ahem, an EPIC sleepover—when she was poisoned by strawberry jelly. Only a jerk would initiate a breakup after a near-death experience, and this boy is no jerk. He's such a good boy that he knows it's not fair to keep things going with his girlfriend, because he has strong feelings for someone else—another girl. Other girl is an implausible object of affection because she could easily be mistaken for a very tall first grader.

OKAY. ENOUGH WITH THE HYPOTHETICALS.

Here's the real deal: Boy is Scotty. Girlfriend is Dori, my ex-BFF from elementary school. Her near-death-by-strawberry experience occurred at a sleepover at *my house*, so boy/Scotty blames *me* for not being allowed to break up with girlfriend/Dori so he can pursue his crush on other girl, who just happens to be—GUESS WHO?!?!—me. As other girl, I should be psyched, right? What seventh-grade girl wouldn't be? This is exactly the sort of juicy situation that turns a Not into a Hot. Being Scotty's girlfriend certainly worked to raise Dori's social profile. But here's the thing: I'm not interested in being Scotty's girlfriend and not only because the position is currently occupied by someone else. It's not Scotty's fault. He's ideal boyfriend material. I'm simply not interested in being his—or anyone else's—girlfriend.

AND THAT'S WHY I'M AFRAID SOMETHING IS WRONG WITH ME.

I watched The Movie. I aced the test afterward. So I know about hormones and how they're responsible for making everything in my body go KABOOM. Occasionally I'll come home from school in a grumpy mood for a legitimate reason, like after Aleck insisted we could make a hot-air balloon out of balsa wood for our Cooperative Woodshop Project, or when Manda and Sara bonked me repeatedly on the head with their inflatable Spirit Squad

5

Squeaky Sticks. Instead of acknowledging that these are valid reasons to be grumpy, my parents blame it on hormones and accuse me of "being hormonal" and complain about barely surviving the "hormonal years" the first time around with my sister a decade ago. But Mom and Dad are wrong. So, so, so wrong. Other than some attention-getting zits, there's zero evidence that my hormones are doing much of anything at all. And that's been perfectly fine with me.

Until big sis Bethany sent me another one of her IT Lists.

Chapter Two

IT List 3
The Guaranteed Guide to stressing,
Obsessing & second-Guessing

1. Early bloomers have it bad.
2. Late bloomers have it worse.
3. Be a middle bloomer.
4. DO. NOT. COMPARE.
5. Remember: No one knows anything.

That's it.

That's *IT*?

My sister still takes pride in being voted Most Popular, Prettiest, and Miss Perfect back in junior high. Since I began seventh grade, Bethany has been duty bound to pass her wisdom on to me. But she's really outdone herself this time around with THE MOST USELESS IT LIST OF THEM ALL. (So far.) Let's review each to-do:

1.   THIS ISN'T EVEN A TO-DO. It's just a statement of opinion. I'd boldly argue that my sister's opinion is WRONG. What's so bad about being ahead of the curves, so to speak? I'd love to get all my growing up (and, um, out) finished before everyone else so I don't waste any more time worrying about when it will happen.

2.   THIS IS *ALSO* NOT A TO-DO. I can at least agree with Bethany on this one. It's no fun being the last girl in the locker room still waiting to develop enough boobage to fill the tiniest training bra.

3.   Okay. This qualifies as a to-do. BUT IT'S TOTALLY NOT DOABLE. I mean, if I had any control over how and when my body would *pubertize* (yes, that's officially a verb now that I've made it up), I'd be over and done with all this crazy body-morphing business already.

4.   Um, let's see. Isn't this tip the complete opposite of what numbers 1–3 are all about? How do I know if I can

"be a middle bloomer" unless I compare myself with the number of girls blooming before (ALL) and after (NONE) I do?

And finally, the fifth piece of nonadvice:

5. I ALREADY KNOW I DON'T KNOW ANYTHING. THAT'S WHY I'M CONSULTING THIS LIST.

There IT is, in all its uselessness. Then again, what did I expect? My sister isn't premed; she's flunking public relations. Sigh. That's the last time I seek health advice from someone majoring in Image Marketing and Management.

So my sister's guide is totally worthless, but I'm glad I didn't trash it in frustration. As it turns out, the flip side could prove to be of much greater value. On the back of Bethany's list is a fascinating document entitled "The Top Secret Pineville Junior High Crushability Quiz."

Sounds like a typical magazine quiz, right? I fill in the little ovals and tally up my results and find out that I'm "Cluelessly Uncrushable" or "Uncrushably Clueless" or whatever. But it isn't that kind of quiz at all.

THE **[TOP SECRET]** PINEVILLE JUNIOR HIGH CRUSHABILITY QUIZ

Directions: Read the question. Open your heart. Write the answer. Face the truth.

Um…okaaaaaay.

Question 1: Are you crushable?

My answer: I don't know. That's why I'm taking this quiz.

Correct answer: Yes, you are! Unless you think you aren't! Then you're not.

My takeaway: This quiz makes no sense and was definitely written by my sister.

Question 2: Do you have a crush right now?

My answer: No.

Correct answer: Yes.

My takeaway: This quiz has no idea what it's talking about.

Question 3: Every seventh-grade girl has a crush. Who's yours?

My answer: I don't have a crush.

Correct answer: Yes, you do!

My takeaway: This quiz is getting on my nerves.

Question 4: Who is your crush?

My answer: Nobody! I've said it two times already!

Correct answer: WHEN YOU LIE, YOU'RE NOT JUST LYING TO ME. YOU'RE LYING TO YOURSELF.

My takeaway: Is it possible this quiz knows things about me I don't even know about myself?

Question 5: Who is the boy you miss most when he's not at school?

My answer: Aleck from Woodshop.

Correct answer: Aha! THIS IS YOUR CRUSH. Even if you answered differently in questions 2-4. DISCUSS THIS IMMEDIATELY WITH YOUR BEST FRIEND.

My takeaway: Wait. What? Whoa.

How did this dumb quiz outsmart me? It didn't play fair. I mean, it didn't ask me to explain WHY I missed Aleck, which is just one of many of the quiz's design flaws. I miss him because he's my partner in Woodshop! That's all! And when he's not there I have to do all the work on our projects, which…well…actually makes it easier to get things done…but, um…well…that's not the point. What is my point? My point is, um, I'm the only girl! And all the other boys are gross! But that doesn't make Aleck my crush! It just means he's the LEAST GROSS OF THE GROSS BOYS.

But…

What if that's the definition of having a crush? After years of thinking all boys are gross, you come across one boy who seems SLIGHTLY LESS GROSS than the others, and HE'S YOUR CRUSH?

Yikes.

IRONY: A quiz attached to an IT List promising to help me stop stressing, obsessing, and second-guessing is now responsible for making me do all three.

Its creator is away at college. I had no choice but to confront her in a phone call.

"I don't understand the Crushability Quiz, Bethany," I complained.

"What's not to understand?" she replied. "It's about as straightforward as such an examination can be and I TOLD YOU TO DROP IT LIKE IT'S HOT."

"Drop, um, what?" I asked, more confused than ever. "I don't remember that being part of the quiz...."

"IT'S LIKE WE DON'T SPEAK THE SAME LANGUAGE."

"Is that why you're yelling at me?"

My sister was making even less sense on the phone than she had in the quiz. But that was no excuse for being shouty. If I were in the mood to get LOUD, I would've read and responded to one of the bazillion ALL-CAPSY!!!! messages Sara had been sending me all morning.

"I'm sorry, Jessie. I'm not talking to you. I'm talking to this SORRY EXCUSE FOR A DANCE TEAM."

"You're on a dance team?" I asked. "When do you have time to be on a dance team? Is this a sorority thing? Shouldn't you be studying?"

My sister spends more time on academic probation than she does off it. In fact, she only recently argued her way back into school after proving she hadn't failed a final but actually passed by three points. If three points were all that stood between me and flunking out of school, you can be sure I wouldn't be spending my time shouting at my sorority sisters to drop it like it's hot. Whatever that even means.

"It's for a good cause. The sorority-fraternity talent show is a fund-raiser for, like, um, world peace or the environment or whatever?"

"You don't know?"

"I am a very busy woman with my social obligations, my sisterhood obligations, my philanthropic obligations, and ARE YOU KIDDING ME? YOU CALL THAT A HIP-HOP PIROUETTE?"

My sister has a lot of obligations at school that don't involve classes, homework, or studying. She effortlessly excels at the stuff that is a mystery to me, which is why I can't stop myself from reading her IT Lists and Crushability Quizzes, accepting whatever advice she gives me even though it always, always, always ends up MESSING WITH MY HEAD.

"And yet despite my hectic schedule, I still pick up the phone to talk to my baby sister. I only wish she had called me with hot gossip instead of calling to complain—once again—about all the helpful advice I've given her."

"But question five—'Who is the boy you miss most when he's not at school?'—was a trick!"

"I take offense to that," Bethany said. "My quiz has been successfully evaluating crushability for more than a decade. I still use a variation of the formula here at college."

Really? That was kind of depressing news. Shouldn't Bethany's sorority sisters have all that boyfriend/girlfriend stuff sorted out by now?

"Kindasorta missing a boy when he doesn't show up for class is not the same as wanting to kiss that boy...."

"Well, in my experience it is. There's a direct connection between missing and kissing. And why are you even calling me about this, anyway? It clearly advises you to discuss this immediately with your best friend and—"

My sister stopped to take a breath, and I thought she was going to scream at the dance team again. Instead her voice got all soft and icky sweet.

"Awww. I get it. I'm sooooo flattered that you think of me as your bestie, but, Jessie, the two of us, we're really bonded by, like, blood and..."

NOTHING ELSE.

I didn't say it and neither did she. But we didn't have

to. It's been pretty much obvious since my birth that we have nothing but our parents in common. Bethany is the embodiment of popularity, prettiness, and perfection. And I'm...whatever I am.

"Anyhoo, you should talk to your best friend about this. Someone who knows you and the boy and can confirm that, yes, you're crushing big-time."

"And then what?" I asked.

"And then you make him your boyfriend, of course."

OF COURSE. And with that final piece of unhelpful advice and a few unmentionable expletives directed at THE MOST DISAPPOINTING DANCE TEAM EVER, my sister hung up.

Okay. So I had to consult my best friend if I hoped to get any clarity on crushability. Who was my best friend these days? Another seemingly simple yet complicated question.

I didn't know if Hope would consider me her best friend, but she was the only person I'd told about Scotty's hallway love confession, and I bet I could trust her with this, too. And if *she* took the quiz, I could compare her answers with mine and...Oh! IT List #4: DO. NOT. COMPARE. But how else was I supposed to know if I'm normal or not?

With no time to waste, I made a quick phone call just to confirm that she was free. Then I hopped on my bike and headed straight for Hope's house.

Chapter Three

I'd never biked to Hope's house before. We went to different elementary schools because her neighborhood is in one zone and mine is in another, even though we're barely a mile apart. As I pedaled down my driveway, I thought about how strange it is that Hope and I have lived within biking distance of each other all our lives but hadn't met until two months ago.

Two months ago, I would've run across the street to Bridget's house, just as I have done thousands of times before. But Bridget and I aren't so close lately. Manda and Sara have accused me of being jealous of Bridget, jealous that she turned pretty overnight, but that's not true. Bridget and I drifted apart not because I envy her, but because of all the ways her new *pretty* appearance has affected every other aspect of her life. Most notably, her dramarama relationship with her boyfriend, Burke. There are only so many false-alarm breakup freak-outs I can pretend to care about. Between Scotty and Dori and Bridget and Burke, is it any wonder I have such a dim view of junior-high romance?

I bet if Bridget had turned pretty overnight but everything else about her had stayed exactly the same, we'd probably still be best friends. And I'm sure our friendship would be stronger than ever if *I* had been the one to undergo some major physical transformation. Like, we'd still be besties if *I* had awoken to two big reasons for trading in my nonsupportive training bralette for an actual bra.

Anyway, I slowed down when I reached Hope's street. She hadn't given me a house number. She'd simply told me to "look for the psychedelic mailbox."

"What does a psychedelic mailbox look like?" I had asked.

Hope laughed. "You'll know it when you see it."

And she was right. I didn't know what I was looking for until I saw what was—unmistakably—a psychedelic mailbox. It was shaped like a dolphin jumping in midair and painted in a neon, tie-dyed/hypercolor camouflage motif. What made the psychedelic mailbox even more unusual was how loudly it contrasted with what was otherwise a totally normal-looking place to live. Like, if the whole yard were zooed out with statues of glow-in-the-dark animals, the psychedelic mailbox wouldn't stand out at all.

Hope was sitting on her front steps next to a large sunken-in pumpkin. The squirrels had gotten to it, chewed through the skin, and exposed the flesh and seedy guts. *That's creepier than any jack-o'-lantern*, I thought. Followed by, *Um, that was a weird thought.*

Hope must have noticed me noticing the pumpkin. Hope is a noticer.

"THE ZOMBIE SQUIRRELS EAT PUMPKIN BRAINS. MWAHAHAHAHAHA."

I laughed, she laughed, and I didn't feel so weird anymore. I mean, I'd *thought* the weird thought, but Hope actually *said* it. Hope's utter unembarrassibility is one of her best qualities.

"You were right," I said, pointing to the psychedelic mailbox. "I knew it when I saw it!"

"Told you so."

Hope went on to explain that she had picked out and hand painted the psychedelic mailbox as a present for her mom's fortieth birthday a few years back. I should have known it was her creation. Hope is artsy like that. She's got an eye for the absurd and the talent to make it work.

"That's so cool," I said, following Hope down a path

that led us from the front to the rear of the house. I hadn't met Hope's parents yet, but I liked them already. I mean, my parents wouldn't use the napkin holder I'd made in Woodshop even when it was just the three of us having dinner. Mom said it clashed with our decor, which I had to admit was true, because my napkin holder is ugly and our house is very tasteful and beige. But still. The making of that hideous napkin holder put several important fingers in jeopardy, and it would be nice to have my dangerous efforts acknowledged. I could only imagine what Mom would think of the psychedelic mailbox. Or worse, the massive plywood skate ramp that dominated the Weavers' backyard. It was covered in illegible graffiti—definitely not Hope's handiwork.

"My brother's," Hope explained.

I heard the sound of wheels scraping cement. A dark mop of hair popped up over the lip of their in-ground swimming pool, then dipped below the surface again. I was too busy watching to pay attention to where I was walking.

"Watch your step!"

Hope threw out her arm to stop me from stepping on the ugliest mutt I'd ever seen. It was also, by all appearances, dead.

"Yikes!" I was more stunned by the creature's hideousness than its deadness.

"Meet our geriatric, narcoleptic Lhasa apso," Hope said. "He only looks dead. He's actually in a very deep sleep."

"He's, um…" I curled my lip. "Ack."

Hope laughed good-naturedly.

"He's a mess, but we love him. He lost a fight with a feral cat, so his face was like that when we picked him out at the shelter, all jumbled up and wrong-looking. That's why we named him Dalí."

"Dalí?"

"Salvador Dalí?" she said. "The surrealist painter?"

I shook my head, and Hope shrugged like name-dropping surrealist painters was no big deal.

"He was twelve years old when we got him, which is eighty-four in dog years, so he already had a different name." She smiled adoringly at her hideous pet. "But Dalí suits him much better than Diamond and he's deaf, so he can't hear what we call him anyway, so we changed it."

Hope was speaking so endearingly about this poor creature that I suddenly felt the urge to show him some love. I bent down to pet him, but Hope grabbed my arm.

"You don't want to wake him," she said. "He will bite your arm off."

I snatched back my hand.

"Yikes! Really?"

"No, not really," Hope said, giggling. "Dalí's missing too many teeth to bite anyone."

My mother would approve a pet velociraptor before she'd ever allow me to bring this pathetic pooch into our home. I was liking Mr. and Mrs. Weaver more and more, but I guess it's easy to like people before you've even met them.

Hope picked up a battered helmet that had been carelessly left on the ground. As we approached the empty pool, we got a better view of her loosey-goosey-limbed sixteen-year-old brother swooping around on his skateboard.

"Heath!" Hope yelled.

Heath was plugged in to music and tuned out to the world. Hope hopped up and down and waved her arms to get her brother's attention.

"HEATH!!!"

Finally, she sat on the lip of the pool and kicked her legs directly in his path. I thought for sure that he'd crash into her, but at the very last second, he shifted his weight to the tail of the board and came to a grinding stop.

"Dude."

"Helmet."

I saw the family resemblance immediately. He was very tall and slender and pale like Hope, with large, expressive eyes. But his shaggy hair was darker and lacked Hope's five-alarm-fire intensity. He wore the typical skater uniform: white T-shirt and baggy, long shorts with holes at the knees.

"Duuuuuuude."

"Helllllllllmet."

"Dude." Heath's whole body slumped. "I hate that thing."

He picked up his board and spun the front wheels with the palm of his hand as if the discussion were over.

"Heath."

I'd never heard her use this sharp tone before. She sounded like a mom. And Heath sounded like a kid four years younger than Hope, not four years older.

"But I wanna feel the wind in my hair...."

"Yeah? And do you want to wake up from a coma with a face like Dalí's, too?"

"Dude."

Hope lowered her gaze and narrowed her eyes, but she didn't speak. Her expression said it all.

"Fiiiiiiiiine," Heath said, dragging himself over to his sister. He took the helmet, reluctantly squeezed it over his head, extended his neck, and snapped the chin strap. Striking a pose, he sought her final approval. "Happy?"

"Ecstatic," Hope replied drily. "This is my new friend, Jessica. We'll be inside."

"Whoa. Whoa. Whoa. Dude."

He held up his hands in protest. Only then did I notice the words written in blue pen on his palms: *RIGHT* and *LEFT*. If Heath were directionally challenged, his notation would only make it worse: He'd written each word on the wrong hand.

"Do you have parental permission to invite New Friend Jessica inside?"

Hope sighed testily as if they had been through this many, many times before.

"It's *your* friends who lost inside-the-house privileges. Not mine."

Heath nodded with mock solemnity.

"Here's a tip, New Friend Jessica." He set one hand down on the board. "Don't jeopardize your inside-the-house privileges by setting our kitchen on fire."

Then Heath kicked off and spun out to the deep end.

Chapter Four

While Hope's head was in the fridge, I surveyed the countertops, cabinets, and appliances, looking for fire damage.

"Did Heath's friends really set your kitchen on fire?"

"Technically, yes." Hope came out holding two cans of Coke. "But it wasn't intentional. Someone put a Hot Pocket in the microwave for thirty minutes instead of thirty seconds and forgot all about it until the explosion."

Before I could stop myself, I asked, "Was it Aleck?"

"Aleck? Who's Aleck?"

Whoops. It's no wonder Hope was confused. Aleck is known as Aleck only in Woodshop because our teacher is bonkers and prefers nicknames to real names.

"I mean Marcus, Marcus Flutie," I clarified. "Didn't you tell me he hangs out with your brother sometimes?"

At first I thought it was a little weird that a high schooler would socialize with a seventh grader. But now that I've actually met Heath—even briefly—I can see how Heath and Aleck might be friends despite their age difference. Hope is waaaaay more mature than her brother. And Aleck would look at the *RIGHT* and *LEFT* on Heath's hands and find a way for it to make perfect sense. Heck. I wouldn't be surprised if Aleck was the one who gave Heath the idea in the first place.

"Oh, right, Woodshop Aleck is Marcus Flutie," Hope said. "Well, that makes sense because if anyone needs an alias, it's him."

"He's getting an F plus in Woodshop."

"Then it should come as no surprise that it *was* Woodshop Aleck who blew up our microwave."

Yikes! What if his failure to correctly set a timer on a microwave indicates an inability to properly operate machinery in general? WOODSHOP IS ALL ABOUT MACHINERY. As his mandatory partner, my life and limbs could be in more danger than they already are! I got so panicky, that Hope felt the need to offer reassurance.

"I might be wrong," she backtracked unconvincingly. "It could have been any one of Heath's friends, really. They're all equally irresponsible."

This didn't make me feel any better.

Hope took a few steps toward the sliding glass door and looked out to the pool. I did, too. The tip of Heath's helmet rose and fell above and below our sight line. Satisfied that her brother wasn't about to crack his head like an egg, she turned back to me.

"Heath and his friends aren't bad people," Hope said diplomatically. "They just make bad choices."

The way Hope said it led me to believe that this was something that got said a lot around the Weaver household. I couldn't help but ask myself: *How many bad choices can you make before you're officially a bad person?* I might have asked for Hope's opinion on that question, then followed it up by introducing her to the Top Secret Pineville Junior High Crushability Quiz, if I hadn't caught a pink blur in my peripheral vision. Hope saw it, too. Our heads turned toward the backyard at the same time.

Ugh. What's she doing here? I thought.

"Ugh. What's she doing here?" Hope said out loud.

Apparently Manda was here to flirt with Hope's brother.

ACK. For several reasons:

1. Manda is Hope's friend.
2. Heath is Hope's brother.
3. Manda is twelve.

4. Heath is sixteen.

5. HEATH IS HOPE'S BROTHER AND MANDA IS TWELVE AND HE IS SIXTEEN.

Manda sat on the steps in the shallow end of the empty pool. She was doing this thing she does, where she arches her back, then leans forward and smooshes her boobs together with her elbows to make them look even bigger than they already are, which is just greedy if you ask me. The maneuver succeeds only if you've got something to work with. OKAY, CONFESSION TIME: I've tried this move at home alone in front of my mirror, and all I've gotten to show for it was a set of bruises where my elbows knocked together. If my sister's IT List mattered at all, I might have worried again about breaking #4: DO. NOT. COMPARE. But it doesn't, so I'm not, so *there*.

While I'm at it, please allow me to use Manda as an example of the bogusness of IT List #1: Early bloomers have it bad. As one of the most advanced girls in our class, you know, developmentwise, she gets noticed by the boys. And she loves it. How do I know this? Because when she *isn't* getting the attention she wants, she goes out of her way to attract it.

Like she did with Heath.

"What's that move called again?" she asked as we made our way outside.

Her voice was pitched an octave higher than usual, which is also something she does when she's talking to boys she thinks are cute, which she does A LOT, even though she's dating Mouth from Woodshop, which is—again—greedy, if you ask me.

"It's the most amazing thing I've ever seen."

She gazed up at Heath through her eyelashes.

"Um. It's just your basic ollie." Heath rolled the board back and forth with his sneaker. "Nothing special. Um. Dude…"

Heath was obviously beyond bored by this conversation with Manda. If he was tolerating her presence at all, it was only because he's a naturally nice person, but that's about it. Even so, Hope looked like she was about to barf all over both of them.

"Hey, Heath!" she said, punching him in the arm. "You remember Manda, who is in seventh grade and the same exact age as your baby sister."

Heath swiveled his head in his sister's direction.

"Dude. Come on. That's nasty. Dude."

"Nasty?" Manda's jaw dropped. "I'm *nasty*?"

"You're not nasty," Heath explained. "I mean, you're not my type or anything. But you aren't nasty."

Manda blinked in disbelief. One. Two. Three times.

"What my sister was hinting at, though," Heath

continued, "like, that I was interested in you in a romantic way? That *is* nasty. Because you're twelve and that's just wrong. Dude."

To sum up: Everyone in the backyard agreed that Manda's flirting was ACK-worthy. Except her, of course.

"WHAAAAAAAT?"

It was a horrible, horrible sound that roused a deaf old dog from his narcoleptic slumber.

"Woof." *Cough.* "Woof." *Cough.* "Woof."

I didn't know dogs coughed.

"This is Dalí in attack mode," Hope whispered helpfully. "He hates Manda. Always has."

"Woof." *Cough.* "Woof."

Dalí limped about as slowly as I've ever seen a four-legged animal go. Manda had plenty of time to carry on with the hysterics until his angry arrival. But before she could screech another syllable, Heath turned up the volume on his headphones and took off for the depths of the deep end. If he heard the rest of Manda's rant over the music, he didn't let on.

"Excuuuuuuse me! You're not my type, either! And I have a boyfriend!"

And then she very emphatically formed a circle with her hand and pumped it in Heath's direction.

"ZERO!" she screeched at the unhearing Heath. "ZEEE-RO."

I didn't understand the meaning of this gesture for sure, but it definitely didn't translate as friendly. Hope knew it, too. We exchanged looks that said, "Let's get her the heck out of here."

"You have some nerve! Like I'd ever go out with a skate rat. Puh-leeze."

"Woof." *Cough.* "Woof."

Pause.

Zzzzzzzz.

I'd hoped Dalí might chase Manda away, but the old mutt had dropped into another dead sleep.

"Some attack dog, huh?" Hope said.

Manda kept "zeroing" one fist in the air as she clutched a sheet of paper with the other. It was getting crushed in her violent grip, but I could still make out the Pineville Junior High Spirit Squad logo at the top of the page. Even though I had my own important piece of paper in my back pocket, the Top Secret Pineville Junior High Crushability Quiz that required Hope's attention, I had to put personal concerns aside for the time being.

"Hey," I said, gesturing toward the document. "Is that a new Spirit Squad petition?"

Hope joined in on the act. Then elevated it to the next level.

"Ooh! A new petition? Come inside and tell us all about it."

31

Manda dropped her "zero" hand and looked down at the crumpled paper.

She and Sara had cofounded the Pineville Junior High Spirit Squad when they were rejected by the Pineville Junior High CHEER TEAM!!! The two clubs are archrivals in pep and popularity. In a few short months, the Spirit Squad has become best known for two things: tight pink T-shirts and petitions. Manda and Sara make it a priority to get a new one going around the school every week. Past petitions include protests against the dress code (because freedom of expression), the vulgarity rule (because freedom of speech), and sloppy joes (because gross). None of these petitions has actually resulted in any changes to school policy—bra straps and four-letter words are still banned, and the cafeteria continues to reek of mystery meat every Thursday—but Manda and Sara insist that they have been very successful at raising awareness.

"And it's an excuse to talk to cute boys we don't know!" Manda has said more than once. LIKE SHE EVEN NEEDS AN EXCUSE.

The point is Spirit Squad petitions were already a big deal. But for Manda to come over to Hope's house on a weekend with a petition in hand? Well, that had to mean this latest protest was the biggest deal of them all.

"We love a good petition, don't we, Jessica?" Hope continued. "Why, I was just saying earlier, the only thing missing from this otherwise perfect day was a good petition. A good petition is the highlight of any week-end, isn't it, Jessica?"

Manda—miraculously—cracked a smile. If I'd shown any snark about official Spirit Squad business, Manda would've told me to shut up—or worse. But Hope has known Manda much longer than I have and can tease the humor out of these tense situations in a way that I cannot. With Manda, I have to be more straightforward.

"What's the Spirit Squad protesting against now?" I asked.

"We're not protesting *against* anything," Manda snapped. "We're protesting *for* something."

"A positive protest," Hope said, coaxing Manda into a standing position. "I love it."

As Hope gently urged Manda toward the house, Heath blissfully circled the drain, totally unaware of all the drama he had created.

Guys. So clueless. And so lucky.

Chapter Five

The three of us gathered in Hope's bedroom to discuss the Spirit Squad's positive protest. I'd never been in Hope's room before, but it felt immediately familiar. Maybe it's because her room is a pure reflection of her personality: It was whimsical without being too wacky.

Hope's curtains were ruby-red velvet, as if pulled from a stage. A chandelier dropped dramatically from the ceiling like a movie star's diamond earring. The desk, chairs, and bookshelves were clear plastic and futuristic and heaped with sketchbooks and art supplies. The rug was a patchwork quilt of scraps cut from different carpets and sewn together. The walls were museum-white, which made sense because they were hung with collages and canvases I assumed were created by Hope herself. It was a lot to take in. And yet the non-matchy-matchiness all came together to make perfect sense.

And this might sound weird, but the room smelled like Hope. Or vice versa, I guess. It's—I don't know—like a mix of wet paint, dried flowers, and fresh laundry with just the teensiest hint of ancient dog. I've always known that I must have a signature smell, too; I just don't know what it is. I can't detect it, because I'm so used to it. This is exactly the type of thing that could keep me awake at night, but I'm friends with Manda and Sara, so I must smell okay. There's no way those two would allow any funky aromas in their inner circle.

(NOTE: This random observation would come back to haunt me with all its irony soon enough.)

Hope flopped onto a mattress on the floor. No bed frame or headboard. Just a mattress draped with an orange-pink-and-white-striped comforter and piled with a bazillion jewel-toned throw pillows. It was lazy and luxurious at the same time. My mother would not approve. At all.

"I like to stretch out," Hope explained.

Hope is already almost six feet tall. How much more can she stretch?

"Oh" was all I could say.

I was kindasorta embarrassed that my mother's

disapproval of floor mattresses had shown up on my face. As a Realtor, Mom likes what sells. Bland, boring spaces have broader appeal to buyers. Hope's chaotic, colorful bedroom was clearly inhabited by someone who is quite comfortable with where—and who—she is. I wish my room could be more like that. My room looks like my mom decorated it. Because she did.

Manda cleared off a space on Hope's desk with a thoughtless sweep of her arm, sending papers, pens, paintbrushes, and a bunch of other stuff tumbling to the floor. If I were Hope, I would have been annoyed. Then again, if I were Hope, I wouldn't have been annoyed, because Hope isn't easily annoyed. It's another one of her best qualities. I get annoyed all too easily.

Manda smoothed out the wrinkled paper, cleared her throat, and positioned herself like an official spokesperson at a press conference.

"Attention!" *[clap clap]* "Attention!"

Manda will literally call for attention when she feels she isn't getting enough attention. She's simultaneously self-confident and insecure in that way.

"Today you have a unique opportunity to be a part of Pineville Junior High history."

She paused so Hope and I could fill the gap with the appropriately awestruck "oooOOOoooh."

"This isn't about a petition," she continued, giving the paper a finger poke. "This is about a rite of passage. This is abou—"

Her speech was interrupted by the sound of the front door banging open and footsteps pounding up the stairs. Judging from the pinched expression on Manda's face, she must have known who it was.

"Oh, puh-leeze," Manda muttered as none other than her BFF and Spirit Squad cofounder breathlessly rushed into the room.

"Sign this!" Sara commanded, thrusting an identical petition at Hope. She saw me a millisecond later. "Aha! Both of you! Yesssss!"

"Hello to you, too, Sara," Hope said archly.

"Omigod." Sara executed an exaggerated curtsy as if she were greeting royalty. "Helllloooooooo." She rose and cocked her hip defiantly. "Happy? Good. Sign this!"

Manda very dramatically cleared her throat. "Ah-he-he-he-he-hemmmmm."

Sara was so focused on us that she hadn't even noticed Manda sitting behind Hope's desk until that moment. She tried not to look surprised.

"Oh, hey, Manda," she said, all supercasual. "What's up?"

"Um, what's up is that Hope and Jessica were just about to sign *my* petition."

"I thought it wasn't a petition," Hope said.

"I thought it was a rite of passage," I said.

Manda has gotten very good at ignoring Hope and me when we team up to annoy her.

"As I was saying," Manda said to Sara, "they were about to sign my petition. So. You know. Tough break, sweetie."

"But they didn't sign it yet."

"We had a verbal agreement."

"Daddy's lawyer will tell you that verbal agreements won't stand up in a court of law, which means…"

Then Manda stunned Sara into silence with the same "zero" hand sign she'd made at Heath. Only this time it had its intended effect.

"Omigod!" Sara cried. "You did not just 'zero' me!"

Manda kept her hand in midair for all to see. She was making it crystal clear that she had, in fact, just "zeroed" Sara and was, for as long as her hand was in midair, still technically "zeroing" her. I still didn't know what it meant to be "zeroed" by Manda, but the pink-to-red-to-purpling of Sara's face indicated that it wasn't very nice.

Ever the peacemaker, Hope stepped between them.

"All this bickering over our signatures," she said, "and we still have no idea what this is all about."

Manda and Sara looked at each other, then us.

"It's for a school dance!"

They said it simultaneously, though from the disappointed looks on their faces it was clear each had tried to beat the other in sharing the news. They still high-fived and said "Bee-Eff-Effs!" to each other like they always did whenever they said the same thing at the same time, but they didn't get much joy out of it.

"Pineville Junior High hasn't had a school dance for, like, a decade," Manda said.

"Omigod," Sara said. "The chaperones complained about too much *quote* inappropriate body contact *unquote* on the dance floor."

I've already established that I get all ACKED out about boy/girl business. So it should be no surprise that the phrase *inappropriate body contact* struck me as way funnier than it should have. At least I wasn't alone.

"Hmmm. Is *this* inappropriate body contact?" Hope asked as she gave herself a piggy nose with the push of her pinkie.

"Is *this* inappropriate body contact?" I asked as I stuck my thumbs in my ears and wiggled my fingers.

"This isn't a joke," Manda said.

"This is, like, serious," Sara said.

This, of course, only egged us on.

Hope bumped her butt into mine.

"Is this inappropriate body contact?" she asked.

I bumped back.

"I don't know," I said. "Is this?"

The next thing I knew, Hope and I were jumping around the room and bumping our butts into whatever—or whoever—got in our way.

"Omigod," Sara said when I butted into her. "You two are so immature."

"Seriously," Manda agreed when Hope butted into her. TELL ME SOMETHING I DON'T KNOW.

When we got bored of bumping our butts, Hope and I crashed onto her mattress, cracking up.

"BWAHAHAHAHAHAHAHAHAHA."

To their credit, Manda and Sara actually waited for us to calm down before trying to communicate with us. We were almost there when Hope very slowly and deliberately reached out and honked my nose twice. Before she could even ask about the inappropriateness of this body contact, we were laughing all over again.

"BWAHAHAHAHAHAHAHAHAHA."

And still, Manda and Sara waited us out. Which gives you an idea of just how important this petition, or rather, this rite of passage, really was to them. Manda cleared her throat.

"Why should we be punished for the mistakes of others made so long ago?" Manda asked.

She approached the problem like a politician. Sara took it way more personally.

"I'm in seventh grade, and I want a school dance," Sara whined. "I deserve a school dance! Gimme a school dance!"

I have a feeling this is the same technique Sara deploys whenever she wants something from her parents. And based on the endless supply of new clothes, new makeup, new gadgets, and new whatever-she-wants, it actually works.

"A school dance could be fun," Hope said in a measured tone. "I'd be willing to support a school dance."

Manda lunged at Hope.

"SIGN MINE!"

Sara lunged at me.

"SIGN MINE!"

I was less enthusiastic about the idea of a school dance because I'm not the most coordinated girl. For me, dancing is a losing mind-body battle between what I think my arms and legs are doing versus what they're actually doing, which is never rhythmic and always a laugh riot to everyone but me. Also, I'm not into dressing up. It's hard enough for me to find five clean T-shirts to wear during the week, let alone a sixth totally different fancy-dancey T-shirt to wear on a Friday night. Finally, school dances inevitably put a LITERAL spotlight on boy/girl business, and you already know how I handle that sort of thing....

This runaway train of thought suddenly brought to mind the paper in my back pocket and the whole reason I rode over to Hope's house in the first place!

I hadn't had a chance to ask her to take the Top Secret Pineville Junior High Crushability Quiz (TTSPJHCQ— an acronym as awkward as I am on the dance floor), and I definitely didn't want to bust it out in front of Manda and Sara, especially when the latter was scrutinizing me in a way that made me feel like a guilty suspect even though I hadn't committed any crime.

"Um," I stammered, unnerved by her stare. "Why does it matter *whose* petition we sign when all the names are for the same cause?"

Manda and Sara looked at me like I was the stupidest person on the planet.

"Let's just say it's a friendly competition," Sara said.

"A best-friendly competition," Manda clarified.

Hope chimed in with over-the-top enthusiasm.

"And you can't spell *competition* without *petition*!"

Without meaning to, we all paused for a mental spell-check. She was right, of course.

"Anyway," Manda continued in a less-than-amused tone, "whoever gets the most signatures by Tuesday morning wins."

"Wins what?" Hope asked. "The comPETITION?"

Now they looked at Hope like *she* was the stupidest person on the planet.

"*Wins,*" they said simultaneously. High five. "Bee-Eff-Effs!"

Hope called me over for a confidential one-on-one conference in the corner next to a shelf of stuffed animals. I never collected stuffed animals. Growing up, that was always Bridget's thing. She used to love adding to her plushy menagerie, but not anymore. When Bridget got a boyfriend, she decided that she was too mature for kitties and unicorns, so she hid them in her closet. I'd bet a bazillion dollars she still sleeps with Miss Petunia Gigglewhiskers.

Anyway, Hope's stuffed animals weren't cute. They were dismembered and sewn back together in bizarre combinations: a hippo head on a teddy bear's belly with duck flippers. Or a bunny face on a fish body with a monkey tail. Frankenplushies.

Hope saw me gawking.

"Salvador Dollies," Hope explained.

Ohhhh. Like the surrealistic painter she mentioned earlier. I swear she has more creativity in her baby toe than I do in my whole body.

"This," she said, thumbing in Manda and Sara's direction, "won't end well."

"It never ends well with those two." Then I corrected myself. "It never *ends* at all. As soon as a winner is declared, the loser will propose a rematch of some sort."

Hope closed her eyes and formed a steeple with her hands in front of her face. It was a show of gratitude. Like, "Finally! Someone understands what I've been dealing with all these years."

Hope spun around to face Manda and Sara.

"Okay! We've come up with a compromise. I'll sign Sara's, and Jessica will sign Manda's."

Not even this, the fairest way of handling the situation, was fair enough.

"Why do you want to sign Manda's?" Sara asked me indignantly.

"Why do you want to sign Sara's?" Manda asked Hope huffily.

"Fine! I'll sign yours and Hope will sign Manda's," I suggested. "It doesn't matter!"

Then I grabbed the pen out of Sara's hand and signed my name to her paper before we could waste another ridiculous second debating the matter any further.

"Are you finally satisfied?" I asked.

Sara inspected my signature, then smiled.

"I *will* be satisfied," she replied, "when you show us what you're hiding in your back pocket."

Mark my words: The FBI will recruit Sara before she graduates from Pineville Junior High School.

"Jess keeps patting her back pocket protectively," she informed the room, "like she's worried something will fall out of it."

"I do?" I asked, genuinely surprised to hear this. I'd had no idea I'd been doing that.

"Omigod, like, at first I thought you were providing more examples of quote inappropriate body contact unquote. Like, pat, pat, pat, pat." She patted her own butt to demonstrate. "But when you didn't actually joke about it, well, I realized it was a tell."

"A tell?" Hope asked.

"A tell," Sara explained, "is body language that reveals the truth."

"Oh, puh-leeze," Manda said dismissively.

"Manda's mouth says she isn't interested in hearing what I have to say," Sara said, all smarty-pantsy, "but the way she leans toward me says, 'tell me more.'"

Manda immediately shifted away to prove otherwise, which only succeeded in reinforcing Sara's point.

"What are some other tells?" Hope asked.

"Omigod. There are zillions," Sara answered. "Nose scratching, half shrugs."

She pointed at my face.

"Lip biting."

I was, at that moment, nervously biting my bottom lip.

"So are you going to surrender what's in your back pocket, or are we going to have to use force?"

"This is all very interesting," I said, "but you're wrong. There's nothing in my back pocket."

"There's nothing in your back pocket?" Sara asked.

I took a deep breath before answering.

"No."

Sara hopped up and down and clapped excitedly.

"Did you see that?" Sara asked Manda and Hope. "She said no, but she nodded *yesssss*."

Both Manda and Hope gave little *aha*s in assent. They had seen it, too.

"I did not!"

"Do you see that? Her arms crossed in a defensive posture? The body doesn't lie...."

THANKS A LOT, BODY.

Now all three of them wouldn't take their eyes off me. They were looking for the truth in my earlobes.

"Stop looking at me!" I snapped.

"Just tell us what you've got hidden back there," Sara said.

"And don't lie," Manda chimed in. "Because I'll know you're lying."

And just like that, Manda had appointed herself the body-language expert in the room. Sara's "you've got to be kidding me" reaction needed no translation.

"If Jessica does have something in her back pocket..." Hope began.

"She does," Sara said confidently.

"Then it's up to her to show it to us or not," Hope continued. "It's her own personal, private business."

"If it's so personal and private," Sara argued, "it should be kept somewhere safe...."

Fortunately for me, Manda has a specific form of attention deficit disorder: She can't tolerate it not being paid to her.

"WHO CARES?!?!" Manda cried out in annoyance. "WE ARE WASTING VALUABLE TIME HERE THAT COULD BE SPENT COLLECTING SIGNATURES FOR A SCHOOL DANCE."

Then she marched through the door without another word. Sara had to make a split-second decision. What mattered more: the comPETITION or my back pocket?

"Wait up!" Sara paused briefly in the doorway to address me. "This investigation is just getting started," she said, as if warning me that she'd return for answers.

Then she chased Manda down the stairs and out the door. Hope and I looked at each other and fainted onto her mattress in relief. We didn't say anything for a few seconds. We just enjoyed the peace and quiet. Quiet and peace. Both are in short supply when Manda and Sara are around.

"So," Hope said finally. "*Are* you hiding something in your back pocket?"

I unfolded my arms and unbit my lip. I emphatically shook my head the correct, negative direction.

"Nope," I lied. "Not at all."

Chapter Six

I should have gotten rid of TTSPJHCQ once and for all when I had the chance.

Shredded it.

Flushed it.

Microwaved it for thirty minutes.

Given it to Dalí as a chew toy.

Even the last option—as impractical as it might have been, considering Dalí has few teeth—would've been better than what I did. Which is nothing at all. Because now the fate of TTSPJHCQ isn't up to me. It's in the least responsible and most mortifying hands possible.

But I'm getting ahead of myself here.

It felt weird to lie about the contents of my back pocket. And the longer I stayed in Hope's room, the more I stressed about her somehow finding out that I had lied, even though the only way that would've happened is if the paper inexplicably came to life, leaped out of my pocket, jumped up and down on the mattress, and yelled, *"LIAR, LIAR, PANTS ON FIRE."*

Why did I lie? Manda and Sara's school-dance drama had worn me out. I didn't have the energy to share and compare notes on TTSPJHCQ anymore, not the way I had when I'd set out on my bike this morning. I figured it would be best to tackle this business another day when I was feeling more up to the task.

The point is I hadn't planned on staying at Hope's too long after Manda and Sara's exit. Ten minutes later, I was waving good-bye and getting back on my bike to pedal home.

"Later!" she said.

"See ya!" I said.

And that's when I heard the barking (and coughing) that should have served as a warning that I was about to get caught in the middle of another battle. But I wasn't paying close enough attention to why Dalí was barking (and coughing) or—more accurately—at what.

It all happened so quickly.

Dog.

Skunk.

DOG. SKUNK.

DOG!!! SKUNK!!!

A bark (cough) and a lift of a black-and-white tail was all it took for this innocent bystander to become a casualty of war.

"AAAAAAAACCCCCCCCCCKKKKKKKKKK!"

Hope screamed almost louder than I did.

Unlike Dalí, I was in motion, so it wasn't a direct hit. But it was still bad, like accidentally walking through a wall of perfume spritzed in the air by those aggressively annoying makeup ladies at the mall with the free samples. It was like that. Except it wasn't perfume imported from Paris; it was POISON EXPORTED FROM A SKUNK'S BUTT.

(NOTE: Remember when I made that random observation about my signature smell? Well, har dee har har on me.)

My mouth must've been open ("SeeyaaaaaAAAACK!") because at first, I tasted the smell more than I actually smelled it. Unsurprisingly, it tasted like something that CAME OUT OF A SKUNK'S BUTT. The smell quickly attacked my nostrils and assaulted my eyes, and a millisecond later I lost control of my bike and wiped out at the bottom of Hope's driveway.

I was blind for what came next. Dalí barking and coughing and Hope yelling "HELLLLLLP!" and Heath yelling "DUUUUUDE!" and a third voice that sounded familiar yelling "I'VE GOT THIS!" but I was too poisoned to think about it much more than that. Someone—I didn't know who—put a plastic jug into my hands, and I poured its entire contents over my face without hesitation. Thankfully, it was water. But it could have been a gallon of milk or gasoline for all I cared. I paid special attention to my eyes and mouth, as if already knowing my nose was probably a lost cause. That smell was stuck. I'd be smelling it for a long, loooooooong time.

After a few minutes, the stinging subsided, and I hesitantly blinked open my eyes.

I saw Hope. I saw Heath, still wearing his helmet.

And I saw Aleck from Woodshop, also wearing a helmet, holding the empty jug of water at his side. YES. THE SAME ALECK FROM WOODSHOP WHOSE NAME I'D WRITTEN DOWN AS THE ANSWER TO DUMB TRICK QUESTION #5 ON THE TOP SECRET PINEVILLE JUNIOR HIGH CRUSHABILITY QUIZ HIDDEN IN MY BACK POCKET.

Go ahead. Take a moment to absorb that information.

Chapter Seven

Okay. Moving on.

"You need to get out of those clothes," Hope said. "Immediately."

Even the mere suggestion of getting undressed in front of two boys got me all flustered because I'm IMMATURE LIKE THAT.

"Um...WHAT?" I stammered.

"She's right. Your clothes are contaminated," Aleck said, "and so are you."

Despite the obvious truth to what he was saying—I was at nuclear wasteland levels of toxicity—I was kind of offended.

"Excuuuuuuuse me?"

"You're wasting time. The longer that stuff has to set in,

the harder it will be to get out." He turned to Hope. "Any chance your mom got a good deal on tomato juice lately?"

"To the stockpile!" Hope said as she dashed into the house.

"The helmet protected most of your hair," Aleck said, appraising me at a safe distance. "That's good. It's hardest to get that stink out of your hair. Especially when you've got a mop like mine."

"So this has happened to you before?" I asked.

"Oh yeah," Heath said. "He's an expert on the subject."

Aleck puffed out his chest.

"I've been sprayed four times," he said.

"FOUR TIMES?" I asked. "What are you, an amateur skunk hunter in your spare time?"

"Yes. When I'm not skateboarding or constructing hot-air balloons out of balsa wood or practicing the ancient Japanese art of origami"—huh, I didn't know he knew origami—"I'm out skunk hunting. But please, give me some credit; I'm a professional."

Hope came running back out with a large can of V8 in one hand and an industrial-strength trash bag in the other. She'd thrown a faded beach towel over her shoulder and clamped a wooden clothespin to her nose.

"We're in luck! There are at least fifty more cans in the stockpile!"

The clothespin made her voice sound all pinched and nasal. Without making a big deal of it, she quietly handed clothespins to Heath and Aleck. They immediately clipped them to their own noses.

"Stockpile?" I asked. "Tomato juice? And why don't I get a clothespin?"

"Our mom is into extreme couponing," Hope explained. "I'll show you the stockpile another time. Right now, we've got to get you out of your clothes and into a tomato-juice tub."

As if the situation hadn't already achieved MAXIMUM LEVELS OF MORTIFICATION, the second mention of getting undressed in front of the boys made me burn even hotter with embarrassment.

"The acidity in the tomato juice neutralizes the skunkiness," Aleck explained. "And you don't get a clothespin because then you're just trapping the odor in your nose."

"Why tomato juice specifically?" I asked. "Why not a more scientific mix of, like, hydrogen peroxide, baking soda, and soap?"

"We always use tomato juice," the three answered. Heath punctuated his sentence with *dude*.

Apparently skunkification was a common occurrence in this neighborhood. That made them the experts, so I deferred to their wisdom. At that point, the stink had totally overtaken my brain, and I couldn't think for myself anyway.

"I'll take you inside the house," Hope said, walking in that direction. "And the boys can hose down Dalí out back."

She stopped me in the garage to hand over the trash bag and the beach towel.

"I'll bring up the cans of tomato juice from the basement. Meanwhile, get undressed, put your clothes in the bag, and seal it tight. *Do not bring it inside!* Understand?"

Hope spoke with the same authoritative tone she'd used earlier with Heath when arguing about the helmet.

"Okay, *Mooooooooooom.*"

I could joke about Hope's momming kind of bossiness, unlike Manda's Spirit Squad business.

"I'll meet you in the bathroom off the kitchen," she said with a smile.

Before doing what Hope asked, I doubled-checked to make sure Aleck and Heath weren't anywhere near the garage. It was easy to keep tabs on them because they were causing a major ruckus. Heath struggled to keep a hold on Dalí.

"Dude, *now* you're wide-awake?" Heath complained to the dog.

Dalí wriggled out of his arms and hit the ground running. Like, actually running.

"I've never seen him go so fast!" Aleck marveled as the two boys took off after him.

I waited until Heath and Aleck were safely out of the yard before stripping down, wrapping the towel around myself, and shoving the noxious clothes into the bag. Upon entering the house, I took extra care not to touch or contaminate anything. When I found the bathroom, I saw Hope had already emptied a few cans of thick orange-red juice into the tub. It looked like a bloodbath straight out of a horror movie.

Hope came into the room juggling a can of juice under one arm, a large candle under the other, and an old-school boom box in her hand. She set the boom box on the floor, the can on the toilet, and the candle on a small shelf above the tub.

"Voilà!" she said, lighting the candle. "Think of it as a high-end spa treatment. I bet Hollywood actresses would pay big money for service like this."

I tried—and failed—to smile at her joke.

"Oh! I almost forgot."

She pressed PLAY, and the bathroom filled with the *plink-plunk-plinky* string plucks my mom calls "relaxation music." Hope waved her hands through the air as if she were conducting the New Agey symphony.

"Well, I guarantee you this," Hope began as she opened

another can and poured it into the tub, "you'll never forget the first—and last—time you came to my house."

I couldn't help but laugh as the juice *glug-glug-glugged* into the tub.

Taking a tomato-juice bath is as gross as you'd imagine. Hope said I needed to sit in the stuff for at least a half hour, after which I'd rinse it all off and take a regular soapy shower. She sat outside the closed bathroom door to give me privacy. While I marinated, she entertained me with stories of her mom's extreme couponing.

"Fifty cans of tomato juice is nothing," she said. "When I was in second grade, I made the mistake of telling her that I liked the Veggie Bears at Sara's house. Remember those? They were gummy bears made out of healthy stuff like spinach and carrots and beets? I was kind of a picky eater, so that was all the incentive my mom needed to use her coupon skills to buy a million billion cases of Veggie Bears for, like, a nickel. We still have a few hundred packages in the stockpile. They're so pumped with preservatives that they never go bad. Ugh. I can't even look at a Veggie Bear without wanting to puke. And when I got my period? Forget it. My mom hoarded enough pads with wings and without wings, for daytime and nighttime, scented and unscented, organic and biodegradable and whatever else to provide feminine hygiene supplies for every girl at Pineville Junior High for the rest of their lives...."

"Present company excluded, of course," I replied from the tub.

"You say that like it's a bad thing."

"Well, when you're the only girl who shows no signs of growing up…"

And just like that, I remembered.

"My pants!" I yelped. "I need my pants!"

I was so set on deskunkification that I'd forgotten all about the Top Secret Pineville Junior High Crushability Quiz with Aleck's name written down as the answer to dumb trick question #5! It was still in the back pocket of the pants I'd hastily stashed in the trash bag! If he found it, I'd never, ever hear the end of it! Teasing me in Woodshop is the highlight of Aleck's goofy, doofy day. And the rest of the Woodshop boys, Cheddar and Squiggy and—oh no!—Mouth, would follow Aleck's lead and get in on the joke, too! Then there'd be no stopping Mouth from busting me in front of his girlfriend, Manda, and she'd—of course!—taunt me in front of Sara and then—*KABOOM!* THE ENTIRE SCHOOL WOULD THINK I HAD A CRUSH ON MY DEMENTED WOODSHOP PARTNER.

This could not happen.

I hopped up from the tub and searched the room for something to change into or cover up with. There was nothing. Hope had even taken away the beach towel for decontamination.

"You can't put those pants back on," Hope said. "I've got fresh clothes for you out here, but you need to rinse off first...."

"I need my pants," I insisted. "Where are my pants?"

"Hmmmm. These pants sound awfully important to you," Hope said. "Like these pants have a deeper significance. It's almost as if these pants are hiding a secret...."

I'd lied to her about not having anything in my back pocket, and Hope knew it. Did she figure it out just then? Or did she know it the entire time and simply choose not to make a big dramatic deal out of it? Either way, confessing the truth at that moment would've been the smart thing to do.

"They're my favorite pants," I lied.

That's right. I picked the not-so-smart option. BLAME MY SKUNKY BRAIN.

"Marcus took the bag," Hope said with a sigh. "He knows how to handle these situations. You can trust him."

And that's how it came to pass that the Top Secret Pineville Junior High Crushability Quiz became the property of the very last person on the planet I wanted to have it.

"So, Aleck, I mean, Marcus," I corrected myself, "will just, like, *destroy* the pants, right? For the good of humankind?"

"Probably," Hope said.

I clung to that *probably* as if it were a rope dangled over a pit of snapping crocodiles wearing pink Spirit Squad

T-shirts. Destruction of TTSPJHCQ was the only life-saving option here.

"After all," Hope continued, "he has a history of setting things on fire."

I could only hope he'd give my pants the Hot Pocket–in-the-microwave treatment.

When my thirty minutes were finally up, I rinsed off, then lathered up with something called Tropical Getaway shower gel that reminded me of another red juice: Hawaiian Punch. After my shower, I changed into a pair of Hope's sweatpants and a T-shirt—both comically too long for me. I took a good whiff of myself, and I honestly couldn't detect the skunk smell anymore. Had the tomato juice successfully removed it? Or had I merely replaced one strong smell with equally strong, if different, smells? Did I now reek like a skunky tomato punch bowl?

I emerged from the bathroom to find Hope at the ready. "The moment of truth," she said. She unclamped the clothespin, leaned in, and sniffed.

She gave me a double thumbs-up.

"You want me to get Heath in here to verify my results?"

I politely declined. As much as I would've loved the opportunity to make Manda jealous ("Heath got close enough to sniff you? WHY DIDN'T HE OFFER TO SNIFF ME?"), just one opinion mattered.

Chapter Eight

Only my extra-sensitive mother could truly determine whether I'd passed the deskunkification test. I rode home quickly, hoping the wind generated at top speeds would aid the airing-out process. When I got there, I headed straight for the home office, otherwise known as the Techno Dojo. I knew my mother would be poring over property listings and buy/sell spreadsheets like she always does after a busy weekend of showing houses. I'd barely stepped into the room before she looked up with an alarmed expression.

"What happened to you?"

She shot up from her chair and headed right to me for inspection.

"What do you mean, what happened to me?" I replied coolly.

"Those aren't your clothes," she said, intimidating me with her eyes. "Why aren't you wearing your own clothes?"

I'd given so much thought to how I smelled that I hadn't considered how I looked.

"Um" was all I said.

"I'm going to ask this only one more time," Mom said sternly. "Why aren't you wearing your own clothes?"

"Um" was all I said again.

When my mom stresses out, she strains all the muscles and tendons in her neck. They looked stretched to the limit, like they could give way at any second, launching her head straight across the room. I knew I'd better come up with a satisfactory answer—and fast.

"Whose. Clothes. Are. They."

"Hope's!" I replied. "They're Hope's."

She held my gaze and wouldn't let go. Sara has nothing on my mother. Mom has a way of looking at me so intensely that I feel like I'm lying even when I'm telling the truth.

"Why are you wearing Hope's clothes?"

"I'm wearing Hope's clothes because..."

I looked down at the shirt in question. It was a souvenir from the Museum of Modern Art gift shop. Inspiration struck. And by inspiration, I mean a lie. Because if I told my mom the truth about the skunk, she'd force me to go through another round of decontamination. There's not enough tomato juice in the world to meet my mom's hygienic standards. I just wasn't up to getting hosed down with Lysol, bathed in bleach, and rolled in potpourri.

"We were working on an art project together. Hope's really creative and crafty, and, well, you know I'm not really any of those things, so I thought it might be fun to give painting a try...."

About halfway through this bogus answer, my mom started to relax. Unlike my sister, who is a frequent truth stretcher, I don't have a history of fabrications undermining my credibility. Mom believed me because I wasn't a liar. Which made me feel pretty terrible about lying to begin with.

"You got paint on the new clothes I just bought you," my mom said knowingly. "And you were afraid to tell me the truth because you thought I'd get upset."

I nodded. It was so much easier when she supplied the lies for me.

She sighed and smiled.

"I think it's wonderful that you're exploring your artistic side," my mother said. "Next time you want to get creative, wear one of those grungy concert T-shirts you found in Bethany's closet."

Much to my mother's dismay, those "grungy" T-shirts were my new favorite articles of clothing. But I wasn't about to press my luck by balking at her suggestion.

"That's a great idea," I said.

Mom lifted her face, and I lowered mine so she could affectionately nuzzle the top of my head. I'd hate it if she ever did it in front of any of my friends, but it's nice when it's just the two of us. It always makes me feel like a kid again, but in a good way. You know. Safe. Taken care of. But my moment of peace came to an end when Mom took a subtle but unmistakable sniff of my hair.

"Something wrong?" I asked.

"Hmm," she murmured vaguely.

"What is it?"

"Make sure you wash up extra well in the shower," she said. "You smell like..."

A SKUNKY TOMATO PUNCH BOWL?

She wrinkled her nose and closed her eyes as if trying to place it.

"Something chemical?" she asked.

"Something chemical," I repeated.

"Paint thinner?" she asked.

I don't know how SKUNK + TOMATO JUICE + TROPICAL GETAWAY SHOWER GEL = PAINT THIN-NER, but I'd take that crazy equation over the simple truth. And I decided right then that's what I'd tell anyone who asked.

"Paint thinner," I replied. "Yes! Because thinning paint

is an important part of painting! Which is what Hope and I were doing today! Painting! Hope and I thinned plenty of paint while we were painting!"

My mother studied me carefully. Her message was clear: "I've got my eye on you." She won't need to look too carefully, though, because I'm the worst liar. Seriously. As Sara so clearly demonstrated, I'm one big tell. In a perfect world, my honesty would be a virtue. And while Pineville Junior High might have been "a perfect world" for my sister, Bethany, it will never, ever be one for me.

Chapter Nine

The next morning, I applied more deodorant than absolutely necessary for a person my size. I hadn't detected any lingering skunkiness, and I seemed to pass my mom's sniff test at breakfast, but still, I wasn't taking any chances. According to my sister's (missing) IT List, no one knows anything. And yet, I do know this: It's a universal truth that no junior-high girl wants to be known as Da Skunkbomb. Though even that might be better than being known as the girl who is crushing on Aleck, because he's got a reputation for being this wild-haired weirdo and WHATEVER! It's irrelevant anyway! Because that dumb TSPJHCQ question #5 *tricked me* into admitting I have a crush on him when I TOTALLY DON'T.

It was way too early for this aggravation. And yet I

wasn't in it alone. Bridget was pacing when I got to the bus stop. Hands clenched. Shoulders squared. Jaw set. It wasn't even eight a.m., and Bridget had already whipped herself up into another frenzy.

"I. Am. So. Mad."

I wasn't expecting mad. Stressed, maybe. Or sad. But not mad.

"Mad? At who?"

With all the girlie drama going on lately, I was half expecting Bridget to say she was mad at me.

"At who? *At who?*" She shook her head in disbelief. "AT BURKE. OF COURSE."

Of course. Only Burke was worthy of such an emotional outburst. And yet... *mad*? This was new. Bridget's never mad at Burke. She's usually worried that he's mad at her for bonkers deal breakers like chewing the wrong flavor of gum or showing up at his locker too soon after the final bell. But he's never really mad at her; it's just her paranoid imagination. Bridget's fury was kind of a welcome variation on the usual bus-stop breakup freak-outs. For the first time ever, she wasn't putting all the blame on herself.

"Why are you mad at Burke?"

She stopped pacing just long enough to kick at the sidewalk in frustration.

"He won't go to the school dance with meeeeee."

"School dance?"

She rolled her eyes. "I know you know about the school dance," she said. "You were the first one to sign Manda's petition."

"I think I signed Sara's petition."

"Manda, Sara, same difference," Bridget said.

This was pretty much true.

"They both showed up at my house yesterday to get me and Dori to sign their petitions."

I should've known that Manda and Sara would go door-to-door with more gritty determination than I'd ever shown as a Girl Scout during cookie-selling season. Nothing would stop them from their goal. Not even kissing up to their enemies.

"And they were all annoying about it, too. Like, 'sign mine, no, sign mine, noooooo, siiiiiiiiign miiiiiiiiiiine.'"

Bridget's dramatization of these events was pitch-perfect. I had to laugh. Then I had to stop laughing because Bridget's frowny face made it clear that none of this was a laughing matter.

"Anyway, the point is there's going to be a school dance!" She did this little skippy hop she does when she's excited. "And that's awesome! Right?"

"Right?"

She stopped and went stone-faced.

"Wrong." She kicked the dirt. "Because my boyfriend is refusing to go with me."

"Why?"

"He said he doesn't 'do dances.' Can you believe that? He doesn't 'do dances.' And I was like, um, you'll 'do dances' when you're my boyfriend, because 'doing dances' is, like, in the boyfriend bylaws."

"Boyfriend bylaws?" I asked. "Is that, like, a real thing?"

There were IT Lists and Crushability Quizzes. Why wouldn't there be Boyfriend Bylaws written somewhere? And you learn the secret location of this information when you become someone's girlfriend. My question was silly enough to make Bridget laugh, even in this dark hour.

"Ha! You can be so dense sometimes! I meant that it's just, like, understood to be something that boyfriends do."

Duh.

"I don't see the point in getting yourself so worked up over something that may not even happen," I said. "Even if Manda and Sara get all the signatures—"

"They'll get all the signatures they need," interrupted Jazmin, the scary eighth-grade goth at our bus stop. When she isn't avoiding sunlight or finding new parts of her body to pierce, she's apparently eavesdropping on all our conversations.

"How do you know?" Bridget asked.

"The girls you were talking about? Manda and Sara? They stopped me on the street yesterday and begged me to sign."

"They asked *you*?" I blurted out.

"Why wouldn't they ask me?"

Jazmin was even creepier when she bared her teeth in her version of a smile.

"Um…" I stammered. "I don't know.…"

Maybe it's because you're totally intimidating with your black hair, black lips, black Sharpie tattoos, black trench coat, black combat boots, black eyes, black SOUL.

I didn't say this, because I don't have a death wish.

"Maybe your friends aren't so quick to stereotype people based on their appearances.…"

I stifled a snort. Manda and Sara weren't being friendly. They just really, really wanted to win. But the bus came around the corner, and Jazmin's civics lesson was brought to a sudden halt because she didn't want anyone to spy her talking to us. Which is ironic, you know, considering Jazmin was just lecturing us about judginess.

Anyway. Usually the arrival of the bus brings Bridget great joy because it means she'll be reunited with Burke in the back seats. Today was not one of those days, however, because Bridget was *mad*.

I took my usual seat in the middle of the bus, and Bridget caught me by surprise by stopping next to me.

"Scooch over!" she insisted. "I'm sitting with you!"

She said it loud enough to be heard by all the boys plugged in to their music in the way back of the bus—Burke included. Now, if Burke were a girl, he might have pretended not to hear her, just like Bridget was pretending not to care if Burke heard or not, which clearly wasn't true, because she kept darting little glances in his direction to confirm that he had heard her. It was an automatic reflex she couldn't control, like blinking or breathing. But Burke isn't a girl. Burke is a boy, and in my limited experience, boys are more direct when it comes to conflict.

"Go to the dance with Jessica," Burke shouted. "I DON'T DO DANCES."

Burke fist-bumped his buddies. Bridget huffed and puffed beside me. A few rows back and across the aisle, Jazmin smiled creepily to herself. All I could do was shake my head in disbelief. How was it possible that so much drama had already been caused by a school dance that wasn't even officially happening?

Yet.

But Manda and Sara had their best people working on it; this much was clear from the moment we arrived at school. Two tables were set up on opposite sides of the school entrance, each displaying banners that could be read from across the parking lot. Manda's read MAKE PINE-VILLE JUNIOR HIGH HISTORY. Sara's read WHO WANTS A SCHOOL DANCE? I DO! Manda's boyfriend, Mouth, and his friends acted as human traffic cones to funnel students in her booth's direction. Sara had recruited the cutest girls on the Spirit Squad to pass out lollipops to lure the crowd her way. It was impossible to tell which strategy was more successful. Both tables were doing brisk business.

Dori was waiting for Bridget in her usual spot in the parking lot. My gut dropped when I saw Scotty wasn't with her. Had he mustered up the courage to break up with Dori so he could be free to pursue his feelings for (ACK) *me*? Feelings he had no business confessing to me in the hallway the other day, because I'm not prepared to return those feelings for him or any other boy NO MATTER WHAT DUMB TRICK QUIZZES SAY.

"I'm SO mad," Dori said.

Gulp.

"What does Scotty mean, 'I don't do dances'?"

"Ugh." Bridget rolled her eyes. "I bet he got that from Burke."

Whew. Their anger had nothing to do with me. And maybe, just maybe, Dori would stay mad enough at Scotty to break up with him before he had a chance to break up with her! Make no mistake: I'm not interested in Scotty in a boy-friend/girlfriend way, but my friendship status with Dori is iffy at best. If the seventh-grade golden couple is doomed, I want the split to have as little to do with me as possible.

"You need to show your boyfriends who's boss," I said to them. "That you won't back down from your principles. That you are committed to this great cause that will undo this great injustice of the past decade...."

"Whoooooooooo!" cheered Bridget.

"Whoooooooooo!" cheered Dori.

I guess my speech worked.

"Imagine how much better the world could be if they channeled this much energy into, oh, I don't know, a worthy cause," Hope said, walking up as Bridget and Dori took off together.

"I was thinking the same thing," I replied. "Like, um, world peace or the environment or whatever?"

Hope gave me a strange look. I was imitating my sister, but she didn't know that.

"That was kind of an inside joke," I explained.

"With yourself?"

"Myself."

"Verrrrry inside."

And with the raise of an eyebrow, Hope turned my inside joke into our inside-out joke. We burst out laughing.

"BWAHAHAHAHAHA."

"You smell good, by the way," Hope said as we entered the school building. "Normal."

"Good," I said, still wondering what "normal" smelled like. But I had more pressing questions to ask. "You ride the bus with Al—I mean, Marcus, right?"

"Yeah," she said. "And you can call him Aleck if that's how you know him. He calls you Clem."

When does he call me Clem? And why?

It's always weird to discover that I am, on occasion, the subject of someone else's conversation. I don't know why. After all, *I* talk about people when they're not around, but I guess I've never considered myself someone worthy of being talked about. Again, I held back on asking for details because I had more important business to take care of first.

"Did he say anything about my pants?" I kept my voice low.

"No," Hope whispered back. "Then again, I didn't ask. You made it pretty clear yesterday that your pants were off-limits."

"Oh," I replied.

I really, really regretted lying to Hope, but it seemed too weird and random to suddenly confess now. And hopefully, if Aleck had done his job, TTSPJHCQ had gone up in smoke, and no one would ever think I have a crush on him because I TOTALLY DON'T.

Hope and I stopped at the intersection of our separate hallways.

"I guess you're just going to have to ask Aleck yourself." She playfully tugged my ponytail. "Good luck with that."

I needed it. I could ask Aleck what he'd done with my pants, of course, but Hope knew as well as I did that there was no guarantee I'd get a straight answer. I didn't want to wait until Woodshop last period to settle this matter, either. Maybe I could run into Aleck before homeroom? I'm *D* for Darling. He's *F* for Flutie. I was willing to make an alphaBET that he was in the homeroom right next door to my own. The challenge, of course, was to wait for him without *looking* like I was waiting for him.

"Gotcha!" Manda and Sara jumped out from behind the opened door to my locker.

Both girls fanned their petition papers in front of their noses, acting awfully chummy for girls so publicly battling it out.

"Are you avoiding us?" Manda asked. "From what we smell, we should be avoiding you!"

"Omigod!" Sara pinched her nose. "You need another tomato-juice bath."

Panicked, without thinking, I stuck my nose in my

armpit. I didn't smell anything skunky. It's clear Sara possesses extraordinary spy senses. Did she pass some of her superior nosiness on to Manda?

Just then, Mouth came up from behind and stuck a completed petition paper in Manda's face.

"Ten more signatures, babe," he said.

"Ten more?" Sara gasped. "Truce over!" Then she set off down the hall.

Mouth noticed me standing there.

"You smell pretty good for someone who just got skunked."

Manda punched him in the arm.

"Why'd you have to tell her?" Manda pouted. "We really had her going."

The warning bell rang for homeroom, and I grabbed Mouth's arm before he could get away.

"How did you find out?" I asked. "About the skunking?"

He shrugged. "Our mutual friend told me."

We have only one mutual friend. And if I didn't know any better, I would've sworn our mutual friend was ditching his homeroom just to avoid me.

Chapter Ten

It was almost funny how fast Sara went from making fun of me to sucking up to me.

"You're tight with the Sampson twins, right?" Sara asked when I took my seat behind her in homeroom.

The Sampson twins and I are friendly from our time together on the cross-country team. But the season is over now, and they've moved on to basketball.

"Sort of." I hesitated. "I guess."

"Omigod! I'll totally have the edge over Manda when you get this thing circulating among the eighth-grade Hots."

"I don't know, Sara."

Whenever we pass in the halls, the Sampson twins still wave and call out "Yo, Notso!" (It's a family nickname: Jessica "Notso" Darling. They'd heard my dad yelling it at our races.) But I didn't feel comfortable claiming to be "tight" with two of the most popular girls in eighth grade. I'm just a little seventh grader. The fact that they're nice to me says a lot about their all-around awesomeness as human beings.

But Sara wasn't taking no for an answer. I kind of admired her tenacity—that is, when I wasn't the one paying for it. She handed me a petition page with her name at the top.

"Get me their signatures, and I'll give you anything you want," Sara promised.

There was only one thing I wanted from Sara: for her to always be as nice to me as she was when she wanted something. But that was as preposterous as asking her to care about the rain forest or the homeless.

"I don't want anything from you," I said.

"Even better!"

She held out her hand for me to shake. And against my better judgment, I shook. It felt easier than not shaking.

"Omigod! My hero! And feel free to get a few dozen more names while you're out there."

And just like that, I was an essential member of Team Sara. I almost worried about how Manda would react to me "choosing" a side that wasn't hers, but I soon came to my senses. No doubt Manda was just as actively drafting soldiers to do her dirty work. Sara had simply gotten to me first because she happens to sit right in front of me in homeroom.

After the bell, I lingered long enough in the doorway to catch all the Fs-through-Js file out of the homeroom next door. When I didn't see Aleck, I assumed he was absent. I trudged to first period, resigned to not knowing the fate of my pants or TTSPJHCQ for another day, at least.

"Did the Sampson twins sign?" Sara asked when I got to Language Arts.

"Um, no."

"Well, how many names did you get, then?"

"None."

"NONE?"

I sighed. "We just got out of homeroom together, like, ninety seconds ago."

"That hasn't stopped me from getting eight signatures in that time...."

She lost all interest in me when Scotty entered the room.

"Scotty!" she shouted. "Sign this!"

Scotty gave her a weary look. "Manda already asked. And I'll tell her the same thing I told you. I don't do dances. No exceptions."

Sara threw up her hands and moved on to her next target.

So there we were, me and Scotty, face-to-face for the first time since he unexpectedly confessed to having a crush on me....

Heeeeey. Hold on a second. Wasn't it possible I'd been mistaken about Scotty's affections? Just as Aleck would get the wrong idea if he saw his name written down as the answer to that dumb trick TSPJHCQ question? Maybe, just maybe, I had misinterpreted Scotty's message. As someone who had come so close herself to being falsely accused of crushing, I was certainly willing to give him the benefit of the doubt.

"Hey, Jess," Scotty said.

"Hey, Scotty," I said.

"Did you hear what I said about not doing dances?" he asked. "No exceptions?"

"Um, yeah, I was right here," I replied.

I did not like where this was going. For a millisecond I'd hoped everything would be normal and totally not awkward between us. But my optimism shut down in the blink of a single eye.

"One exception," he said quietly.

AND THEN HE WINKED AT ME, AND I TOTALLY ACKED OUT.

"No," I said firmly.

"Yes."

"NO."

"YES."

Noooooooo! I am not crushable! I don't know the meaning of *crushable*, which is why I took that dumb quiz in the first place!

Obviously Scotty was—is—mistaken. Maybe he took too many hits to the head during football season. Speaking from experience, there's only so much traumatic impact a developing brain can take before things get a little bonkers in there. How could I prove to him that I'm not the crushable type so he'd get back to the business of being Dori's devoted boyfriend and stop ACKing me out with these ambush declarations of crush? Without any evidence to back me up, all I could do was try to talk him out of it. But too many students were filing into the classroom, and it was not the time nor the place for a conversation like that.

"No," I said with finality as I took my seat.

Honestly, if it were up to me, the ideal time and place for a conversation like that would be NEVER and NOWHERE. I was desperate for a distraction and so grateful when Hope staggered into the room with a petition in her hand. It had Manda's name on it.

"I don't know how it happened...." Hope said in a daze. "One second Manda was apologizing for showing up at my house unannounced yesterday, and the next second I'm on a mission to get signatures from all the skaters by the end of the day."

I held up Sara's sheet. No explanation necessary.

"We know better than to get involved in their drama," Hope said. "We're smarter than this."

Hope's no dummy and neither am I. More often than not, schoolwork comes fairly easily to me. And I enjoy the challenge of mastering academic concepts I don't get at first glance. But when it comes to the girlie head games at which Manda and Sara excel, I'm flunking out.

"We're smarter than this," Hope repeated, as if trying to convince herself.

I patted Hope sympathetically on the shoulder.

"Apparently not."

So the rest of our day was spent in pursuit of signatures because Hope and I are clearly not as smart as we'd like to think we are. The funny thing is, getting names isn't nearly as hard or as awkward as I thought it would be. Word had quickly gotten around about Manda and Sara's mission, and most students were psyched to sign up. In fact, when I held the petition facing up and out so everyone could see it as I walked around, I didn't have to do any asking. It was quite the opposite, really.

"Yo, Notso!" Shandi Sampson called out to me in the hall after first period. "You got room for me on that thing?"

"Me too!" chimed in her twin, Shauna.

"Of course I've got room for you two," I replied, "and the rest of the girls' basketball team...."

I had similar exchanges after second period with Padma and the drama club and after third period with Molly and the boys on the wrestling team. As stupid as this whole comPETITION between Manda and Sara was, I must admit to feeling a little thrill of victory when I slapped my paper down on Sara's desk at the start of fourth period.

"Mission accomplished," I said proudly. "With four periods left to go."

"Omigod!" Sara snatched up the list and quickly scanned the names. "You did it! You got the Sampson twins and the entire girls' basketball team and—"

"Turn it over," I told her.

Because I'd filled up more than the allotted twenty-five spots, the last dozen or so names had been added to the back. Sara's eyes widened with surprise.

"Omigod! There's no way Manda can wi—"

Sara hushed herself when Manda waltzed into the room, with Hope trailing behind.

"I got the Future Farmers of America!" Manda bragged. "I recognized them as an untapped market."

"Actually, I did," Hope interjected, which made sense

because I couldn't imagine Manda going out of her way to talk to anyone who prefers pigs to people.

"Wowwww," Sara said in fake admiration. "That's, like, three signatures. How will I ever catch up?"

When Manda turned her back to us, Sara gave me a triumphant double thumbs-up.

Chapter Eleven

I was minding my own business in Woodshop, paging through a workbook of potential projects, when I was startled by a loud snort in my ear.

"You pass the smell test!" Aleck announced cheerfully.

"You!" I barked. "Where have you been?"

"I've been..."

And he spun his hands all through the air as if to say "everywhere."

Act normal, I told myself. *He didn't see his name written in your handwriting as the answer to dumb trick question #5. ACT NORMAL. There's nothing to worry about. He knows nothing. ACT NORMAL!!!*

I decided ACTING NORMAL!!! in this case required the use of sarcasm.

"Thanks a lot for telling everyone that I'd been skunked."

"You're welcome. I believe public awareness is the first step in destigmatizing the plight of the skunked, don't you?"

On another day I might have laughed along or encouraged him to start a petition of his own. But I couldn't be all carefree until I knew for sure what had happened to my pants and—more importantly—its contents.

"I need to talk to you," I said.

"We're talking now," he said.

"It's"—I lowered my voice—"a confidential matter."

Aleck rubbed his hands together.

"A confidential matter!"

It was embarrassing enough I had to ask Aleck this question. The least I could do was try to minimize my mortification by preventing anyone else from hearing. I motioned for him to come closer. He took this as a sign to take another loud, deep sniff.

"You smell fine," he assured me. "I swear."

"It's not about that," I said. "Where are my pants?"

Just my luck that at the same exact moment, someone in the workshop turned on a buzz saw.

"WHAAAAAT?" Aleck shouted over the *BZZZZZZ*.

"MY PANTS," I shouted back. "WH—"

The buzz saw shut off...

"WHERE ARE MY PANTS?"

...just in time for the entire workshop to hear me shout the question.

Of course.

Need I remind you that I am the only girl in a classroom full of boys? They don't need much of an excuse to launch into a collective fit of immaturity. I'm surprised only when their jokes aren't made at *my* expense.

"Aleck, what is it with you and girls' pants?" shouted Mouth.

"Did you outgrow the purple corduroys?" shouted Cheddar.

Aleck, as usual, was unfazed.

"One time in fourth grade, I showed up at school wearing the same pair of purple corduroys as your good friend Sara D'Abruzzi."

He said it with a shrug, as casually as could be.

It was weird to hear Aleck describe my relationship with Sara in such chummy terms. Is that what people thought? That Sara is my "good friend"? One double thumbs-up does not equal a "good friend."

"Anyway," he continued, "my friends love giving me crap about it. And you just gave them a perfect opportunity. So thanks."

"You've got nice legs. Next time try a skirt!" shouted Mouth.

"My sister will take you shopping for leggings!" shouted Cheddar.

Aleck heroically ignored his friends' taunts.

"So," Aleck said, "you have concerns about your pants?"

"They're my favorite pants," I lied.

"Then I'm sorry to report that the pants have been destroyed," he said apologetically. "For the good of noses everywhere."

"Ohhhh…" I said.

"Ohhhh, what?"

"I didn't empty out my pockets before I put my pants in the bag, so…"

"Hmm." He raised an eyebrow. "Did you lose something important?"

I answered quickly. "Nope! Nope! Nope!"

On my third *Nope!* I realized I was nodding my head yes instead of shaking it no, a classic tell, according to Sara. When I yanked my head back and forth to overcorrect my mistake, I nearly gave myself whiplash.

"NOPE!" I said once more.

Aleck smiled and clapped me on the shoulder.

"Good news for you, then," Aleck said brightly. "I didn't find what you never lost."

And he swaggered back over to his buddies with a shocking degree of confidence for someone who'd spend the next fifty minutes as the butt of their cross-dressing jokes.

So if Aleck was to be believed, the Top Secret Pineville Junior High Crushability Quiz was gone for good. But no matter how hard I tried, it was definitely not forgotten.

Chapter Twelve

I was at my locker the next morning before homeroom when Sara ecstatically rushed up to me.

"Omigod! I did it! I won! I got thirty-seven more signatures than Manda!" she shrieked. "Mr. Masters confirmed it this morning when I dropped by his office!"

Thirty-seven. What a coincidence. That's the exact number of names I'd single-handedly gotten for Sara. I knew it would be far too much to ask Sara to acknowledge any role I played in her victory, so I didn't even bother. Besides, the dance isn't as big a deal to me as it is to her. I just wanted her to keep being nice to me for a change.

"So what exactly did you win, anyway?" I asked.

Sara giggled deliriously.

"First of all, I beat Manda! I won! I'm the winner! Second of all, I'm in charge of the dance committee! Not her!"

As BFF of the self-appointed Boss of Everything, Sara has very few opportunities to be in charge of *anything*. It's no wonder she wanted to win so badly.

"Omigod! Mr. Masters said he's going to make a major announcement this morning!" She hopped up and down with excitement. "A MAJOR ANNOUNCEMENT!"

"About the dance?" I asked.

"No," she snapped. "About the honor roll."

"But Mr. Masters already announced the honor roll."

I knew this because I was on it. And when Sara rolled her eyes, I also knew I'd just allowed my Nerd Self to get ahead of my Trying to Be Normal Self. Again.

"OF COURSE ABOUT THE DANCE."

"Of course," I said.

"So you're with me on the committee, right? You have to be on the committee. I won't take no for an answer."

"I don't know," I said. "I'm not the dance-committee type."

"Think of it as an opportunity to show support for your school," she said. "And besides, what else do you have to do after school, now that you're not running around in the woods anymore?"

She had a point there. Unlike my cross-country teammates, I didn't have a new activity to fill my afternoons now that the season was over. The Sampson twins tried to encourage me to try out for the basketball team until they saw for themselves that I can't dribble and move my legs at the same time. Molly is breaking new ground as the only girl on the boys' wrestling team, but I have zero interest in appearing in public wearing a spandex unitard. And humming a terribly out-of-tune "Happy Birthday" was the only explanation Padma needed for why I wouldn't try out for the school musical.

At first, I welcomed the opportunity to come home right after school. I thought more free time would equal less stress. I quickly discovered that more free time equals more opportunities for my parents to fill it with things I don't want to do.

"Jessie! You're not doing anything! Chop these onions!"

"Jessie! You're not doing anything! Take out the trash!"

"Jessie! You're not doing anything! BE OUR SERVANT WITHOUT A RAISE IN YOUR ALLOWANCE."

Jessie needed to find something to do. And fast. And how much worse could it be than crying over the cutting board and dragging stanky garbage cans? Maybe—like cross-country—being on a dance committee would be something I'm surprisingly good at. Because I'm not at all emotionally invested in the school dance, I could be the most impartial member of the committee and make decisions unclouded by my own personal interests. Who knows how many CEOs got their start on school-dance committees?

"Okay," I said to Sara. "I'll do it."

"Omigod! This is going to be the best."

"What's going to be the best?" asked Manda, who had slipped in between us.

"Oh, you know," Sara said, "chairing the dance committee with Jessica as my second-in-command."

"Jessica? As your cochair? Ha! Good luck!"

Manda was usually very good at "I don't care" hair tosses. But it was obvious to Sara and me that she cared very, very much.

"Come on, Jess," Sara said, linking my arm in hers and escorting me past Manda. "I can't wait to share my vision for the dance."

And during the short walk to homeroom, Sara shared her vision for the dance, which apparently was no longer a school dance at all but an extravagant ball.

"It's called"—she paused dramatically—"the Glamarama Gala."

And so began a breathless monologue that included phrases like *black-and-white dress code* and *floor-length formals* and *tuxedos* and *crystal accents* and *orchids and roses and lilies* and *silver carpet not red carpet because red can be so harsh in photos....*

"Um" was all I could say. "Well."

"Omigod! It's the best vision ever!" She twirled a curl around her finger. "Unless you have a vision you'd like to share?"

I obviously hadn't given much thought to my vision, since I'd been on the dance committee for a grand total of two minutes. But that's not to say I didn't have an idea or two.

"Well," I began hesitantly, "that sounds really... ambitious."

"What's wrong with ambitious?" Sara said defensively.

"It's just that something, I don't know, *simpler* might be more..."

"More what?" Sara said huffily. "BORING?"

"It's the first dance in a decade, right?" I started slowly, then quickly gained momentum. My brain works that way sometimes. "I'm thinking it could be cool to acknowledge that this is an important part of Pineville Junior High history, you know? Maybe give it, like, a retro theme and decorate with old yearbook pictures and stuff. We could call it Friday-Night Flashback."

Judging from the repulsed look on Sara's face, I either: (a) had just come up with the worst idea she'd ever heard or (b) still reeked of skunk.

"What is it with your obsession with ancient stuff?" she said, gesturing toward my R.E.M. *Green* T-shirt as we took our seats. "No, my idea is definitely better, and it will make things go a lot faster if you just agree with me."

That was my first indication that Sara wanted me on the committee to conspire—not contribute.

"Good morning, students. This morning I'm pleased to make a very special announcement," said our school principal, Mr. Masters, over the PA system.

"Omigod!" Sara grabbed me by the arm. "This is it!"

"Thanks to the devoted efforts of the Pineville Junior High Spirit Squad…"

She squeezed hard.

"Omigod! That's me!" She looked around the room to make sure everyone heard her. "That's *me*, everybody!"

"I'm happy to announce that a week from Friday, Pineville Junior High will host its first school dance in ten years."

Cheers erupted from all over the building. Sara jumped out of her seat.

"You're welcome, world!"

The class applauded as she took her bows. Tears of joy shone in her eyes. I'd never seen her like this before, so thoroughly proud of herself. It was like she was the first person in history to win an Academy Award and the Powerball jackpot on the same day.

Our principal continued.

"The Down-Home Harvest Dance will be a unique opportunity for all Pineville Junior High students to practice and perform the celebrated folk art of square dancing."

Square dancing? I asked myself.

"Square dancing?" asked 399 Pineville Junior High students.

"Yes, square dancing," Mr. Masters replied, as if answering all four hundred of us directly.

"SQUARE DANCING?" Sara tugged angrily on her earlobe, as if to dislodge the terrible thing she had just heard. "Omigod! I didn't work so hard for SQUARE DANCING."

"Square dancing," said Mr. Armbruster appreciatively. "There's nothing quite like a good do-si-do."

Sara brazenly risked a detention by grabbing a bathroom pass off Mr. Armbruster's desk without asking and stomping out of the room in a huff. Apparently he was too caught up in memories of do-si-dos from days gone by to do much about her insubordination.

"Bow to yer partner," he was saying to himself. "Bow to yer corner."

Well, I thought, *at least one person is excited about the Down-Home Harvest Dance.*

Sara never showed up for first period. But Manda did. And boy, did she look pleased with herself as she galloped into Language Arts twirling an imaginary lasso.

"Howdy, pardners!" she said in a country-girl accent. "Giddyap!"

She laughed hysterically at her own joke, then—*crack!* like a whip!—got dead serious.

"I have nothing to do with this ridiculous square dance," Manda said to no one and everyone at the same time. "Ask Sara. She's the one who got all the signatures."

Manda wasn't wasting any time distancing herself from what she assumed would be a social disaster.

"The whole concept is lame," Manda said. "What's Pineville known for harvesting, anyway?"

"Drama," Hope said.

Now *that* was funny.

To be honest, I was with Mr. Masters on this. The only dancing I can do that resembles actual dancing is the kind of dancing with specific rules. So, like, the Electric Slide is my jam. Square dancing is all about rules. As a concept, it seems far less terrifying than a freestyle free-for-all. Not that I'm actually attending the dance. I might help Sara plan it, but that doesn't mean I'll show up for it.

Sara reappeared during second period. Apparently she'd spent the first half of Language Arts trying to persuade Mr. Masters to come to his senses. But he was unmoved. To him, the Down-Home Harvest Dance is a perfect compromise. We get a dance, but a highly structured one with very specific rules guaranteeing a lack of "inappropriate body contact." Win-win.

"It'll be the most glamorous *square dance*"—Sara choked on the words a little—"Pineville Junior High has ever seen!"

"That's because it will be the only square dance Pineville Junior High has ever seen," Manda replied. "Oh, and good luck getting anyone to show up when no one even knows how to do-si-do."

Then Manda swung her imaginary lasso and yeehawed away from us.

Sara appeared untroubled by the fact that not a single Pineville Junior High student knew how to square-dance. As second-in-command, I felt duty bound to discuss the pitfalls of our situation.

"Manda has a valid point," I said to Sara. "No one will come to a square dance if they don't know how to square-dance."

Sara removed a book from her backpack and held it up for me to see. Who knew our library had a copy of *Square Dancing for Dummies*?

"Oh, they'll *learn* how to square-dance."

As Sara already knew—and we would discover for ourselves in sixth period—that's what gym class was for. And our gym teacher, Mr. Wall, was not happy about it.

Chapter Thirteen

I am not a big fan of Mr. Wall.

The first reason isn't really his fault: I hate gym class no matter who teaches it. One kickball to the face in first grade was all it took for me to develop skepticism for all sports. (Upside to the trauma: A wiggly-but-stubborn tooth popped out on impact, and I got a fiver from the tooth fairy.) It hasn't gotten much better as I've gotten older. As I've explained, with the exception of running, I'm not the most coordinated person. I feel like I'm put together wrong and weird like one of Hope's Frankenplushies: all rubbery octopus arms and wobbly baby-giraffe legs with the head of a blind mole rat. Even the least dangerous activities like yoga or Ping-Pong become life-and-death situations.

Plus, it's a hassle changing out of my regular clothes

and into my regulation PJHS gym apparel. And the gymnasium is always hot and humid, like the planet's sweatiest, stankiest rain forest. Worst of all, jocks like Scotty take gym class more seriously than all their other classes combined. They get all hyped up and gladiatorial and *RRRRAWR!!!* and it's really, really unpleasant for the rest of us who are just trying to get through the next thirty minutes without becoming collateral damage in their BLOODY KICKBALL BATTLE TO THE DEATH.

But I suspect their over-the-top intensity has a lot to do with Mr. Wall's teaching style. *Teaching* isn't the right word. It's more like *bullying*. As coach of the Pineville Junior High football team, he treats each gym-class activity as if it is the Super Bowl. And I mean *every* activity, including yoga and Ping-Pong. And, evidently, square dancing.

"PARTNER UP, YOU LAZYBONES!"

He reminded me of my sister yelling at the dance team. Up to that moment, I'd never noticed the similarities between Mr. Wall's and Bethany's insult-ridden motivational tactics.

"WHADDYA GOT, WAX IN YOUR EARS?"

Now that football season is over, he's the coach of the wrestling team. Which brings me to the second reason I don't like Mr. Wall: He totally tried to stop my friend Molly from going out for the team. He was all like, *Oh, she's just a little girl. She'll get slaughtered, and her parents will sue the school, and blah blah blah.* He obviously didn't know who he was dealing with. Molly's tiny but tough. And she's a girl of few words, but when she speaks up, she makes them count. So she was like, *Title IX, Mr. Wall. Supreme Court says I have the legal right to try out.* And she did. And guess what? She totally pinned the little dude in her weight class, and it was a victory for girls everywhere, and hooray feminism!

"I SAID PARTNER UP, YOU."

There are about thirty of us in this gym class. It's mostly students from the Gifted & Talented classes, with a few randoms thrown in just to make things interesting. Partnering up is kind of standard. Like, one person does the sit-ups, and the other person holds her feet and counts. Or one gets her wobbly baby-giraffe legs pretzeled up in lotus pose, and the other gets her unstuck. Or one hits a Ping-Pong ball, and the other swings and misses with all eight of her rubbery octopus arms and takes it right in the blind eye.

You know. FOR EXAMPLE.

Usually I'm with Hope, but sometimes we'll end up splitting Sara and Manda if they're in a fight and refuse to partner with each other. With all of Manda's giddyapping about the Down-Home Harvest Dance, it looked like today was one of those days. I acknowledged the situation with a simple nod to Hope. She returned the nod and sidled up to Manda as I approached Sara.

"Looks like it's you and me," I said as the rest of the class shifted around to stand next to their usual gym partners.

"Not so fast," Sara said.

Mr. Wall was shaking his head in misery.

"Not THOSE types of partners," he shouted. "PARTNERS partners!"

This still wasn't making any sense to anyone but Sara.

"Boys with girls! Girls with boys!"

Because we weren't getting the point, Mr. Wall grabbed the nearest boy by the back of his PJHS gym shirt and shoved him in the direction of the nearest girl.

"For square dancing!"

Sara smiled. But the rest of us didn't move a muscle.

"Get moving! You've got thirty seconds to pick your partners, or I'll pick them for you." He clicked the stopwatch he always wears around his neck. "GO."

The next thirty seconds were as harrowing as any I've ever experienced. And this is coming from someone who was once chased by a giant goose who wanted to make me his girlfriend. But that lovesick bird was nowhere near as terrifying as the person who came after me in the gym.

"You and me," Scotty said, grabbing my hand.

I yanked it back and slapped him on the wrist.

"No way!"

"You've got to partner up with someone; it might as well be me," he said. "And Dori isn't in this gym class, so..."

And then he winked.

ACK. HE WINKED. WHAT'S WITH SCOTTY AND ALL THE WINKING?

All around me, couples were coming together: Mouth isn't in our gym class, so Manda put aside her negative attitude about square dancing long enough to make a beeline for Scotty's cute friend Vinnie. Sara targeted a quiet kid named Sam who wouldn't even try to interrupt her endless chatter. Hope pointed at Mike, the tallest boy on the basketball team, who responded with a comic "Who, me?" pantomime, as if their pairing hadn't been inevitable all along.

My options were running low with every second that ticked by. Pretty soon, it would be down to Scotty and this kid John-John, who *always* has a runny nose and *always* wipes it on the back of his hand. What would be worse? Being on the receiving end of Scotty's winks or John-John's snot? So help me, I went with the winks. But not without a stern warning.

"Don't get any ideas," I said.

"I never have any ideas," Scotty replied.

I used to think that was true. That Scotty was one

hundred percent pure jock and nothing else was going on in his head besides, like, fart jokes and *RAWR!!!* But I was discovering that Scotty has lots of ideas in his head. Many about me. AND I DON'T LIKE THOSE IDEAS ONE BIT.

"You've got ten seconds to find three other couples and make a square." Mr. Wall pressed the stopwatch and blew the whistle. "GO."

I assumed this would be easier. The obvious square was me and Scotty, Hope and Mike, Sara and Sam, Manda and Vinnie. But Sara was having no part of any square that included Manda as one of its sides.

"Omigod! No!" she said. "You don't want this dance to happen! You will not sabotage my square!"

"Oh, puh-leeze. Like I even care enough to sabotage your square."

"You do and you will," Sara shot back. "And I won't let that happen!"

"FIVE SECONDS," warned Mr. Wall.

"Scouts!" Sara shouted at a pair nearby. "You're with us!"

Everyone calls them the Scouts. I don't even know their real names. He's a Boy Scout and she's a Girl Scout; they wear their full uniforms to school sometimes. This is something nobody—and I mean NOBODY—else does, which is ironic because wearing uniforms is usually, like, a sign of conformity. (I just imagined Hope saying, "You can't spell *conformity* without *uniform*!" This isn't accurate, but you get the idea, right?) I've often wondered if the Scouts genuinely like each other or if they felt obligated to start a junior-high romance based solely on their matching uniforms. Either way, the Scouts joined our square without hesitation, because they're used to following orders.

Manda was livid.

"Fine!" she shouted. "I'll put my own square together!"

"No time for that," Mr. Wall said. Then he steered her by the shoulders over to a triangle that needed a fourth pair to complete their square. Vinnie followed. I don't like playing into Pineville Junior High's popularity stereotypes, but there's no question in my mind that Manda categorized those three couples as the nottiest of Nots.

"Oh no! We're not going alone!" Manda dug in her heels. "Hope's coming with us!"

Mr. Wall blew the whistle. Time was up. Hope looked at Manda and held up her hands in a way that was supposed to look like "sorry" but came closer to "*whew*." She stayed put.

"The squares stand," Mr. Wall pronounced, as if there were any question in the matter.

"Heeeeeey, everyone!" Sara called across the gym triumphantly, loud enough for the entire class to hear. "How can a square also be a circle?"

It was unlike Sara to pose a mathematical riddle. But it would be even more unlike me not to answer.

"It can't," I replied automatically. "In fact, the phrase *squaring the circle* is a metaphor for an impossible problem. It goes back to the ancient Greeks—"

"Gee, thanks, Einstein," Sara said, cutting me off. "A square is a circle when—"

"Euclid," I corrected. "As in Euclidian geometry."

I honestly don't even know how I know these things sometimes. I just do. I read a lot, I guess. And my dad is also a big nerd. THANKS, GENETICS!

"Omigod! Nerd alert! You're killing the joke!"

Then Sara raised her hand in the air to deliver the punch line: She "zeroed" Manda's square.

There's no way everyone in the gym knew what it meant. And yet EVERYONE IN THE GYM KNEW *EXACTLY* WHAT IT MEANT.

If you know what I mean.

Manda's response was furious and swift. She fought back with a defiant hand—or rather, *finger*—gesture of her own. One that definitely did not comply with the vulgarity rule.

"OMIGOD. MR. WALL, DID YOU SEE THAT?"

Of course Mr. Wall saw it. We *all* saw it. To make sure no one missed it, Manda did a full 360-degree rotation. Yes, a perfect circle within the square.

Chapter Fourteen

Manda spent the rest of the class in the principal's office. Her absence loomed large over the gymnasium. Everyone was too busy buzzing about her obscene gesture to concentrate on the square-dance lesson our gym teacher didn't care if we learned anyway. He was still shouting at us, but without his usual enthusiasm.

"Square up, slackers! Boys to the left, girls on the right!"

Simple enough. Scotty was already standing to my left. I quickly looked away before he could wink at me in congratulations of our superior square-formation skills. You think I'm joking. I'M NOT. This simple direction was apparently far too complicated for the rest of the class to handle because I swear about a bazillion years went by before every person in every square was standing in his or her proper spot.

Mr. Wall slumped on the sidelines, put his head in his hands, and moaned.

"This is not why I got a degree in exercise physiology."

"She's sabotaging the dance, and she isn't even here!" Sara fumed.

It was true. With the flip of a finger, Manda had turned our do-si-dos into do-si-HECK-NOS. No doubt this is exactly what she'd had in mind. Sensing a crisis in the making, Sara took over.

"Listen up, numskulls," Sara yelled. "You're gonna learn how to promenade your partner OR ELSE."

This was her own special interpretation of the rough-and-tough teaching technique favored by Mr. Wall and my sister. With *Square Dancing for Dummies* as her guide, Sara spent the rest of the time bossing us around while our gym teacher barely looked up from his issue of *Sports Illustrated*.

"Bow to your partner!"

Sara faced Sam and bowed. I faced Scotty and bowed. Everyone faced everyone and bowed.

"Bow to your corner!"

Sara turned right. All the girls turned right. Sam also turned right. All the boys turned right. This was WRONG.

"No, you dipsticks! Boys turn left! Boys' corner is on the left!"

And then she forcibly grabbed and spun poor Sam so he faced left. All the girls forcibly grabbed and spun their poor partners so they faced left. Except me. Because Scotty looked all too eager to be grabbed by me.

"I think you can handle that move on your own, buddy."

Meanwhile, on the opposite side of the square, Hope cautiously tried to get Sara's attention.

"Excuse me, Sara?" she asked politely. "I'm thinking that maybe it might be easier to learn the moves if we had some music...."

Sara went off like a firecracker.

"Music? You two-left-footed nincompoops can't handle music! I'll tell you when you're ready for music!" She pumped her copy of *Square Dancing for Dummies* into the air above her head. "Until then, the only music you clumsy nitwits need is the *SWEET SOUND OF MY VOICE*."

At full volume, Sara can make the ceiling quake. Mr. Wall looked up briefly from his magazine, yawned, then went back to it.

"Where was I?" Sara scrunched her curls, smoothed out her shorts, and composed herself. "Oh yes! Swing your partners. Like this!"

Then Sara manipulated Sam like a mannequin into the proper arm-in-arm position and swung him around.

So all the girls took the boys by the arms and swung them around.

The Scouts were naturals. Hope and Mike were a perfect match, too, but comically out of proportion with all other sides of the square. They practically bent themselves in half whenever a call required them to trade partners with any of the rest of us, a move Hope quickly dubbed the "Hunchback at the Hoedown."

As for me and Scotty...

"OW!"

We bonked heads during the bow to your partner.

"Sorry!"

"OWW!"

I jammed an elbow into his rib during the allemande left.

"Sorry!"

"OWWW!"

I knuckled him in the chest during the right and left grand.

"Sorry!"

I was sorry, too. Mostly. I mean, I wasn't hurting him on purpose. I really was the clumsiest nitwit in a gym full of clumsy nitwits. And yet I couldn't help but think that maybe all this negative reinforcement might get him to see that I'm not the girl for him after all. If I caused him enough physical pain, maybe he'd come to associate me with emotional pain. If I'm crushable, it's because I'm the crush*er* not the crush*ee.*

"OWWWW!"

Um, literally.

"If this keeps up," he said, rubbing his neck where I'd clipped him during a swing-around-and-round, "I'll need my helmet and shoulder pads!"

I listened for a hint of annoyance in his voice, any sign that he was getting sick of me and wanted to trade me in for a less dangerous partner. But Scotty didn't sound the least bit irritated. And when he laughed out loud, he was showing me—and everyone else in the gym—just what a good sport and a great guy he really was.

Ugh.

At the time, I thought that was the most annoying thing he could possibly do. But then he got even more annoying during lunch. I was hiding a few spots behind him and Dori on the cafeteria line, but I was just close enough to watch him show off all his square-dance injuries for his girlfriend.

"If I didn't know any better," he joked, "I'd think Jessica was trying to kill me."

Dori's eyes narrowed to slits.

"*Jesssssica?*" She really hissed those *s*'s. "Jessica was your partner?"

I opened my milk, popped in a straw, and took a sip. I thought this made me look more casual and less like I was hanging on to every word.

"Yeah," Scotty replied, as unconcerned as could possibly be.

Dori glared. Crossed her arms. Tapped her foot. Waited. I'm totally clueless about crushability and boy/girl business, but even *I* could see what Dori wanted out of Scotty at that moment. I wanted to shout at him.

ASK HER.

"Tater Tots today?" Scotty asked. "Or fries?"

NOOOO! ASK HER WHO HER PARTNER WAS. DORI HAD GYM THIS MORNING, TOO. SHE WANTS YOU TO BE AS JEALOUS AS SHE IS.

"Don't you want to know who my partner was? Aren't you the least bit curious?"

Scotty paused, looking pensive.

"I can't decide."

"You can't decide...what?"

After a second's hesitation, Scotty put Tater Tots *and* fries on his tray. He grinned at his good decision, turned to Dori, and finally spoke.

"Um. What were you saying?"

Dori slammed her plastic tray on the metal counter.

"My partner was Marcus Flutie!"

Wait. What? Whoa. Seriously? Of all the boys in the entire school? It had to be Marcus Flutie aka Woodshop Aleck? WHAT THE HECK?

"And he's a much better dancer than you are!"

As Dori stomped away, it was clear to me that her announcement had succeeded in triggering maybe, just maybe, the teeny-tiniest twinge of jealousy.

Just not in the intended target.

"Huh," Scotty said, watching her go. Then he wordlessly pumped ketchup onto his tray full of fried potato products.

Meanwhile, my hands were shaking. The open carton rattled on my tray, spilling milk over the edge and splashing into a puddle at my feet.

What a mess, I thought.

Fortunately, I had a few minutes left in the lunch period to get myself together before Woodshop. The Top Secret Pineville Junior High Crushability Quiz had tricked me into confessing a secret crush on my demented Woodshop partner. But merely saying something doesn't make it true. Duh. Look, I'll prove it right now: My boobs are bigger than Manda's.

Let's check.

Nope. Still flat as a board.

So despite the truth about my nonexistent crush on

Aleck, I still couldn't explain why I had a physical reaction to Dori's news. That is, until I heard Manda's explanation for what happened in the gym.

Oh yeah, she was in her regular spot, right next to Sara at our lunch table. The two of them were dipping carrot and celery sticks into a shared container of ranch dressing, all la-di-da no-biggie besties, business as usual. I was the only one who thought there was anything strange about getting sprung so quickly from the principal's office.

"I thought you'd be getting tased right about now," I said to Manda. "You know, for breaking the vulgarity rule."

"Oh, puh-leeze."

She rolled her eyes and slid a piece of paper across the table.

"I've got a doctor's note excusing any dramatic changes in behavior on account of the uncontrollable and unpredictable hormonal fluctuations associated with adolescent development."

Sure enough, that's exactly what it said in a letter signed by a doctor whose name I couldn't read because he—like all doctors—apparently flunked handwriting in elementary school.

"It's the PMS defense," Hope explained.

"See, that's where you have it all wrong," Manda said.

"This letter excuses bad behavior in the pre-, post-, and mid-menstrual times of the month."

"It's brilliant," Sara said. "It grants Manda permission to be a total nightmare whenever she wants to be for, like, ever."

"You make it sound like I have a choice in the matter." Manda made her eyes all wide and innocent. "It's a chemical imbalance. I can't control my actions. I'm a victim of my raging hormones."

"*We're* victims of your raging hormones," Hope muttered just loud enough for me to hear.

"Whatever," Sara said skeptically. "I want one of those letters."

Even I'd learned early on in junior high how making vague complaints about "girl stuff" could get you excused from any classroom with few or no questions. But Manda had really taken it to the next level with an official letter.

"You don't really believe hormones are to blame for Manda giving Sara the finger, do you?" Hope asked me.

"No," I replied. "Of course not."

That's what I said. But it's not one hundred percent what I believed. I mean, maybe there was a little bit of truth to the doctor's letter. Perhaps all these crazy hormones are making it hard for any of us to take control of our emotions. Our *actions*. I mean, if a chemical imbalance was responsible for Manda flipping Sara the bird, why couldn't it also be the reason why my hands shook the tray, spilled the milk, and made the mess?

According to at least one medical professional, I wasn't suffering from jealousy.

I was suffering from puberty.

Chapter Fifteen

With puberty as my excuse, I was feeling much better about the Dori/Aleck square-dance situation when I got to Woodshop. Unfortunately, my Woodshop teacher did not share my chipper mood. Mr. Pudel slumped against his desk and read dejectedly from a school memo in his hands.

"It seems that for the next two weeks we're putting our regular curriculum aside to pursue…ah…" He looked down at the paper. *"An exploration of the celebrational ornamentation most commonly associated with folkloric traditions combining movement and musicianship."*

None of us had any idea what he was talking about. He crumpled up the paper and tossed it in the nearby trash can.

"We're in charge of making decorations for the Down-Home Harvest Dance."

Oh.

"The administration uses fancy terminology like that so it gets credited as an academic activity," he explained.

Ohhh.

"EVEN WHEN IT'S A BIG BUNCH OF HOOEY."

Sara chose that moment of all moments to sweep into the room.

"Yoo-hoo!"

"Who are you, and why are you in my workshop?" Mr. Pudel asked.

"I'm Sara D'Abruzzi, and—"

Mr. Pudel cut her off.

"Listen, Bruiser, you have no business in my workshop."

Sara came up only to the chest pocket of Mr. Pudel's lumberjack shirt. But if she was intimidated by his menacing growl, or the boys' goggle-eyed gawking because they couldn't believe there was an *actual girl* in their classroom (I stopped registering as an *actual girl* ages ago), she didn't show it.

"I do when I'm the chair of the dance committee," she said confidently. "And here's my dream decor that you need to make a reality!"

She went straight to the drafting table and fanned out

several pieces of graph paper, the kind with the tiny boxes I use in Pre-Algebra to chart x- and y-axis problems.

"What are those?" Mr. Pudel asked.

"Construction and design plans, of course!"

Between the disruption of his teaching schedule and Sara's intrusion, Mr. Pudel looked angry enough to flip over the table and everything on it. But when he got close enough to give Sara's papers a quick glance, he...stopped. He calmed down.

"You did these?" he asked, picking one up for closer inspection.

"Omigod! Of course!"

I peeked over Sara's shoulder to get a look. I couldn't see much, but I could tell that Mr. Pudel was pretty impressed with Sara's plans, despite his best efforts not to be.

"I approve of this project," he said. "Bruiser, you may stay."

"My name is Sara D'—"

"Not while you're in here, it isn't," Mr. Pudel said. "Explain how things work, Clem."

Then he rustled up Cheddar and Squiggy for a trip to the supply closet. They'd take stock of what we had and what we needed for the project.

"When did you do these?" I asked, after taking a better look at her drawings.

"During Social Studies," she said casually. "And Science."

Her sketches were way more detailed than I assumed they would be, with all the measurements and dimensions and suggested materials and everything. There were instructions for a plywood barn facade, silhouettes of farm animals, a post-and-rail fence, and all sorts of other good ol' country stuff like that.

"How'd you learn how to do this?" I asked.

"We always have contractors working on our house." She shrugged. "I've remodeled my bathroom, like, three times."

I had no idea Sara had such a talent. And if Manda had gotten more signatures and won the comPETITION, I never would have found out. It pleased me to have played a role in Sara's success—even if she reciprocated by treating me like her personal slave.

"Jess! Round up the hotties for heavy lifting!" she said. "I need big muscles!"

And that's the moment that Aleck and Mouth chose to saunter into the room. Ten minutes late, I might add.

"You called for us?" Aleck said.

Aleck and Mouth are many things, but strong and brawny aren't two of them.

"Omigod, you have, like, one muscle," she said. "Combined!"

Sara immediately set her sights on the jocks and put them to work hauling plywood out of the supply closet. Without anything constructive to do, Aleck, Mouth, and I just kind of stood around awkwardly.

"So," I said.

"So," Aleck said.

"Burp," Mouth said.

Fascinating.

"Did you hear how your girlfriend got herself out of detention?" I asked Mouth.

"I know!" Mouth said, getting all keyed up. "Girl stuff! It's so unfair!"

"It's discrimination," Aleck agreed.

"Why can't I blame my stupid behavior on guy stuff?" Mouth asked. "I've got hormones, too, you know."

"So we smell," Aleck said, plugging his nose with one hand and waving the air around Mouth's armpit with the other. "Didn't you pay attention to Nurse Fleet's lecture? 'Deodorant. Use it!'"

"That's it," Mouth said, straddling his stool. "I'm getting a note from my doctor. I'll never get detention again."

"Not so fast," Mr. Pudel said as he slapped two detention slips down on the table. "That's the third tardy for both of you. Automatic detention."

"But, Mr. Pudel," Mouth protested. "Hormones!"

Mouth hopped up and followed our teacher to the supply closet, taking three quick steps for every one of his.

"So why were you late for class, anyway?" I asked Aleck. "Were you getting extra square-dancing practice with Dori?"

ACK.

I don't want to get in the habit of blaming hormones for every little stupid thing I do. Especially when there's very little evidence that my hormones are doing much of anything. But without them as an excuse, I can't really explain what made me say that. I mean, who cares who Aleck is paired with? Me getting weird about Aleck dancing with Dori makes even less sense than Dori getting weird about Scotty dancing with me, because she at least has a boyfriend/girlfriendship at stake. Aleck and I are mandatory Woodshop partners. That's it. And yet I've felt sorta awkward around Aleck ever since TTSPJHCQ falsely accused me of having a crush on him. I can't shake the feeling that he knows. NOT THAT THERE'S ANYTHING TO KNOW.

You know?

"We don't need extra practice." Aleck grinned. "We're that good."

"Oh, really?"

"Yes, really."

"Well, my partner and I are really good, too," I lied. "The best."

I waited for Aleck to ask who my partner was, but he didn't. He just smiled to himself and said nothing. I snapped like Dori on the lunch line, for no good reason.

"What?!"

"I find it hard to believe that anyone is better than me and Dori," Aleck replied. "And our superior skills elevate the rest of our square to another level of excellence."

"Is that so?" butted in Sara.

Literally. She smacked me in the behind with a large roll of graphite tracing paper. I hadn't even noticed that she was close enough to listen in on our conversation. No wonder she always hears gossip before anyone else.

"It is so," Aleck said.

"We'll see," Sara said. "At the Hoedown Showdown."

"The what?" Aleck and I asked.

"The Down-Home Harvest Dance championship," Sara said, setting the roll on the table. "You can't have a square dance without declaring a winning square!"

Of course not. Because everything's a competition to Sara.

"And we *will* win." Sara picked up an X-Acto knife. "Won't we, Jessica?"

"Do-si-do!"

It wasn't a yes or a no, but it satisfied Sara nonetheless.

This definitely wasn't the time to tell her that I have no plans to actually attend the dance. Not with so much on the line. Another *W* in Sara's column would mean an *L* in Manda's. I couldn't predict how that revised ratio of victories and defeats would level the popularity playing field at Pineville Junior High. But as Sara's cochair and one-eighth of her square, I have a front-row VIP pass to all the action.

Whether I want it or not.

Chapter Sixteen

Later that night, my parents and I were eating organic sprouted multigrain pasta with Tofurky mini meatballs for dinner. Or rather, I was *trying* to eat. My mother's efforts to cook all healthy always result in food fakes that taste nothing like the original dishes they're pretending to be. I spiked a shell and sniffed. Ack. It smelled like something you'd find clinging to the underside of a rotting log.

"Your dad and I feel bad that we've been so busy lately," Mom said, picking at her salad.

"Uh-huh," I said, dumping a pound of Parmesan cheese on the all-natural nastiness on my plate.

"We know you weren't happy about being ba—" Mom cut herself off before saying *babysat*. "I mean, *supervised* by Gladdie."

"But work has calmed down considerably for both of us," Dad added, reaching for the cheese when I was done.

My dad does technical support for a school district, so the first few months of the academic year are a crazy time for him, because everyone forgets how to use their computers after returning from summer vacation. And though my mom sells most of her houses in June, July, and August, she gets bogged down with all the related paperwork through early fall. They were so worried about not having enough parental guidance that they actually persuaded my grandmother Gladdie to watch over me for a couple of weeks or so. At first I was offended that they got me a babysitter because they still see me as a baby and not an almost teenager. But spending those weeks with Gladdie was pretty sweet in every sense of the word. First, no one bakes like she does. And because she's old she's got, like, wisdom, and she helped me out with a lot of my girlie drama. I was sad to see my grandmother go back to Florida, but I'd never admit this to my parents. Know-it-all parents are the most annoying parents.

"We want to make it up to you," Mom said.

Hey! If they wanted to believe I deserved a reward for enduring my time with Gladdie, I wasn't going to correct them. I tried to act all casual about it because my parents always make too much of a big deal whenever I get excited about anything.

"Um, okay," I said.

"We want to do something special," Dad said.

"A once-in-a-lifetime thing," Mom said.

There was only one once-in-a-lifetime thing I could think of.

"Holy koala!" I shouted. "We're going to Australia!"

I've been obsessed with the smallest continent since I was about four and learned that it's summer in Australia when it's winter in New Jersey because it's located all topsy-turvy in a whole different hemisphere. And then I started reading up on Australia and was wowed by the fact that so much of its animal population—kangaroos! koalas! and that krazy platypus!—isn't found anywhere else in the world. I wouldn't be surprised if one of Hope's Frankenplushies was discovered there someday. Anyway, I've always considered Australia the Land of Opposites and Misfits. This appealed to me long before junior high made me feel that way on a regular basis.

The point is I couldn't act all supercasual about Australia.

"Omigod! Australia! Omigod! Australia!"

I reminded myself a little bit of Sara in that moment. Had we been spending too much time together lately? My parents kind of looked at each other like, "oops."

"We aren't going to Australia," Dad said.

"Ohhhh."

I was deflated but not entirely defeated. I dared to guess again.

"California? Omigod! California!"

Yikes! More of my inner Sara was coming out. This scared me. And that fear launched my Nerd Self into hyperdrive.

"I've always dreamed of going there before the next great earthquake sends the California peninsula floating into and around the Pacific Ocean," I babbled. "But then again, if I wait long enough, California could eventually drift far enough to become part of Australia and I could visit both places at the same time...."

AND MY TRYING TO BE NORMAL SELF WAS DEFEATED ONCE AGAIN.

"We're not going on a trip, Jessie," Dad said.

"We're not?"

"Why travel," Mom said, "when we can spend quality time together much closer to home?"

I liked the sound of this less and less.

"How close to home?" I asked. "New York City? Philly?"

I made the mistake of popping a mini meatball into my mouth.

"The Down-Home Harvest Dance!" my mom said.

"Your mother signed us up to be chaperones," my dad said.

"Won't that be fun?" my mom said.

And then my dad slapped me on the back a few times because I was choking on a half-chewed wad of Tofurky.

"How did you even find out about the dance?" I asked when I finally recovered.

"Parents are e-mailed a weekly newsletter to keep us informed of school happenings," Mom said. "And it's a good thing, too; otherwise we wouldn't know anything!"

"Well, I'm not even going to the dance."

I had it all figured out: I'd stay home. Scotty would draft Dori to fill my spot. Poor Aleck would be left without a new partner and unable to wow the judges with his allegedly superior square-dancing skills. Sara would win the Hoedown Showdown, and everyone would be happy. Well, except Manda. And Aleck. But I wasn't about to lose any sleep over that.

"You have to go!" my mom said. "You're the cochair of the dance committee! You've made a commitment!"

"I'm in the newsletter?"

"Yes," Mom replied with pride. "With specific mention of your Industrial-Arts connections."

"My *what*?"

I pushed my plate away and headed straight for the Techno Dojo to read this newsletter. Sure enough, before "Girl Wrestler Invokes Title IX" (yay, Molly!) and after

"Sloppy Joes Stay on the Menu" (boo, Spirit Squad!) was "PJHS to Hold First Dance in a Decade." There's no doubt where the information came from. Only Sara would think to write a press release for a junior-high dance, incorporating phrases like *square-dance chic* and *haute couture country* and *putting the prom back in promenade.* (She definitely stole that last bit of wordplay from Hope.) I was surprised Sara had credited me at all. And it was exactly as my mom had said. I was "the dance cochair with Industrial-Arts connections." Yep. That's me, all right.

I spun around in the swivel chair and faced my parents.

"You really, really don't have to go to this dance...."

"We want to go!" my mother said.

"Your mother wants to go," my father corrected.

"You wanted to support her cross-country meets, so..."

"So your mother feels we should support this, too."

Mom pointed an accusatory finger at Dad.

"And if you had chaperoned Bethany's junior-high dances back in the day," she snapped, "you'd understand why I think it's important for us to be there now."

"Notso isn't Bethany."

It's always awkward when my parents get snippy in front of me. But it's the cringiest when they get snippy in front of me *about* me.

"You're the techie one! You know kids grow up so much

faster these days because of the Internet! If you'd seen what I saw on that dance floor ten years ago, you'd shudder to think what Jessie's class is up to!"

The truth slowly dawned on me.

"Waaaait," I said. "Was Bethany's class the last one to have a dance?"

"Yes," my mother said. "And with good reason. There was a lot of…"

Her voice trailed off as she struggled for the right phrase. Fortunately—or not—I could fill it in for her. But could I say it without falling into a fit of giggles?

"There was a lot of"—I took a breath to brace myself—"inappropriate body conta-hahahahahahahaha?"

Nope. I could not say it without laughing. It was a valiant effort, though. I made it all the way to the last syllable of the third word before breaking down. And I wasn't the only one losing it. My mom's face flushed pink. My dad's bald head got all sweaty. I think they were more embarrassed by where this conversation was going than I was.

"You have nothing to worry about!" I informed them. "It's a square dance specifically approved by the administration to reduce opportunities for inappropriate bo-hahahahahahaha."

That time I didn't even make it past the first syllable of the second word. This was probably for the best, though, because my parents were visibly relieved by my display of immaturity.

"You're right," Mom said to my dad. "She's not Bethany."

And I swear, for the first time in my life, my mother wasn't saying that like it was a bad thing. She was saying it like she was relieved.

"It's settled, then!" I said, clapping my hands together. "You don't have to go!"

My parents' eyes met. "Oh yes, we do," they said together.

I'd blown it. I knew it as soon as the words had escaped my mouth. I'd made their nonattendance sound too important to me.

Now that they're going to the dance, I'll have no choice but to attend, too. Because the only thing worse than seeing your parents embarrass themselves in front of your classmates is NOT seeing your parents embarrass themselves in front of your classmates and having to hear all about it afterward in excruciating, exaggerated detail.

"It'll be fun!" Mom said.

"Yippee-ki-yi-yay," I said, unenthused.

"Yeehaw," my dad said, also unenthused.

I must admit that I felt just the teensiest little bit better knowing someone in my family dreads the idea of a school dance as much as I do. THANKS, GENETICS!

Only this time, I'm not being sarcastic about my gratitude.

Chapter Seventeen

One thing I'll say about Sara: She won't hesitate to join forces with foes to get what she wants. But I never, ever could have imagined a scenario that would find her sharing earbuds with cranky old Mr. Armbruster.

And yet that's exactly what I came upon when I walked into homeroom the next day. Sara was slapping the top of his desk in time with the music I couldn't hear.

Mr. Armbruster was tapping the same beat with his foot. Both were smiling. SMILING. I hadn't seen him smile since that time he found out I was on the cross-country team and had to tell me all about his epic race against the legendary Kicky McGhee.

But there he was. Smiling. With Sara. And sharing her earbuds.

I felt all topsy-turvy. Like Australia.

Sara noticed me gawking and called me over. Literally, as in square-dance style.

"One leg, a-two leg, a-three leg, four," she half sang, half twanged. *"Promenade across the floor!"*

Mr. Armbruster made "tsk-tsk" fingers and corrected her gently. "It's not a proper promenade without a partner."

"Mr. Armbruster here is certified by the International Square Dance Association!" Sara bragged. "A total pro!"

Apparently Sara had brought in song selections to get Mr. Armbruster's opinion. He was all too eager to lose himself in the banjo, fiddle, and washtub bass.

"He's given you detention, like, six times," I whispered in her free ear. "I don't think he likes you very much."

"Omigod! He hates me," Sara whispered back cheerfully. "But he loves square dancing!"

That was an understatement. This unlikely duo spent the rest of homeroom—and the rest of the week!—discussing the merits and drawbacks of traditional versus Appalachian versus modern Western styles of square dancing. Needless to say, Sara easily recruited him to be the official caller of the Pineville Junior High Down-Home Harvest Dance. And Mr. Armbruster had no problem freeing up his teaching schedule to make calls during our gym-class rehearsals, which makes me wonder what dubious educational contributions he's making to Pineville Junior High when he isn't telling us to *circle left* and *circle right* and *pass through* and *separate* and *split two* and *roll away....*

That's square dancing: a blur of commands and sweaty, sweaty hands. At least Scotty is courteous enough to dry off his palms on the front of his jeans. I'd thank him, but any time I initiate even the tiniest bit of conversation, he interprets that as an invitation for one of his WINKS. Fortunately, square dancing is all about listening and following Mr. Armbruster's directions. So it's pretty much impossible to carry on a casual conversation while you're doing it. Especially on Sara's watch.

"So, Jessica, what—"

"SILENCE IN THE SQUARE."

"But—"

"SILENCE."

Sara is more determined than ever to win the Hoedown Showdown. She had effectively eliminated Manda by exiling her to the misfit square. To no one's surprise, Manda got another doctor's note that officially dismissed her from the competition for *medical reasons.*

"Teen-Onset Extra-Sensitivity Disorder," she had explained to me and Hope in Social Studies. "I am negatively affected by loud music and unexpected movement."

As I've said, Hope is superhumanly unannoyable. But Manda's latest excuse was too much even for her to take.

"That's a made-up diagnosis!" she blurted. "And you're not even a teenager!"

"I'm an early bloomer," Manda replied before strutting off to Study Hall instead of gym class.

"Do you think she believes her own lies?" Hope asked when she was gone.

"I think," I said, "she believes whatever she wants to believe."

"But how does she persuade everyone else to go along with her?"

Hope has known Manda longer than any of us—since preschool. If she didn't know the answer to that question, I was certain no one did. And I would've said so if Sara hadn't blown a whistle in our faces.

"Stop yer gabbing! Get to the gym! We've got a Hoedown Showdown to win!"

I hate to admit it, but Sara's coaching is working. Every day we are getting better. The eight of us picked up the moves much faster than any of the other groups. I only occasionally clock Scotty with an elbow or knee, and yet I'm still almost as sore from square dancing as I'd been during my first weeks of cross-country practice. It doesn't make sense to me.

"Does square dancing make your back ache?" I asked Sara as we traced the outline of a cow on a piece of particle board in Woodshop. "Mine is killing me."

"Get your act together!" Sara reprimanded. "No excuses!"

She stood up and brusquely marched across the room to check on a wooden horse in progress. That's when Aleck took it upon himself to give me some unsolicited advice.

"It's not the moves," he said. "It's how you're doing them."

"Excuse me?"

"It's all the tension in your body. You hold yourself all rigid, like Scotty is about to electrocute you. It's no wonder your muscles hurt."

Okay. I'm willing to admit that he was right. Yes, it's true I can't relax around Scotty, because AS I'VE MENTIONED, whenever I let my guard down he gets all winky with me. But I stopped myself short of congratulating Aleck on this observation.

"Are you spying on me?" I asked. "Is that how you know what I look like when I'm square dancing? Because that's—"

Aleck interrupted my accusations.

"Squiggle dancing."

I had to repeat this out loud, just to make sure I'd heard him correctly.

"Squiggle dancing?"

"That's what I call it," he said. "Squiggle dancing is square dancing with wiggle room for creative interpretation."

"Wiggle room? For interpretation? Sara goes ballistic when our elbows don't jut from our sides at perfect forty-five-degree angles when swinging our partners."

"And that by-the-protractor approach to square dancing is why you are going to lose and we are going to win."

"Aha! So you *have* been spying on me?"

In truly annoying Aleck fashion, he didn't confirm or deny. He simply smiled all knowingly.

"Just loosen up. Trust me. It will be more fun and less stressful on your body."

Then he swung his arms all around as if he were twirling two jump ropes at once.

"See how loose I am?" he asked. "Fun!"

As he solo double-Dutched himself to the back of the workshop, I thought about all the fun I wasn't having because I'm stuck in Sara's square instead of his.

And then I thought about how this lesson is the sort of thing I miss out on when Aleck doesn't come to class.

And then, finally, I thought about why I'd written his name down for dumb trick question #5 and how I was really, really relieved he'd destroyed the Top Secret Pineville Junior High Crushability Quiz before anyone had a chance to see it.

My feelings for Aleck are too complex for such a dumb test.

Chapter Eighteen

Saturday mornings are for sleeping. Except today.

"Jessie!" My mother knocked on my headboard. "Your friend is downstairs waiting for you."

"Who?" I rasped. "What?"

And before I even opened my eyes, I got my answer.

"Omigod!" Sara yanked away my duvet and flung it to the floor. "We're going shopping for dance dresses!"

"When?"

"Right now!"

A horn honked in my driveway to illustrate her point.

"Come on, my brother won't wait for long!" She pulled on my arm. "It's a good thing you go for the natural look. No one will even notice you just woke up!"

I pulled a pair of jeans off the floor and put on the

T-shirt at the top of my basket of clean laundry. Sara literally pushed me out the door and down the stairs.

"What's the rush? The mall isn't going anywhere, is it?"

"Um, no. But any dress worth having will be gone before you can say 'Daddy's Amex'!"

She flashed what I assumed was her father's American Express card.

For the record, I didn't have my parents' plastic. I had eleven dollars balled up in my front pocket. And it was a ten and a single, so I couldn't even pretend to be flush with cash. The only place I could afford to splurge was Cinnabon. This, by the way, got my vote for the first stop on our shopping trip because Sara had dragged me out the door without any breakfast. She didn't even let me put my sneakers on. I was still barefoot when she shoved me into the backseat next to a bunch of shopping bags. Sara slid in beside me and started shouting commands at the teenage boy behind the wheel. Or rather, teenage *man*. He had a beard.

"To the mall! In a hurry!"

"Yes, your majesty," the teenage man replied sarcastically, tugging on the brim of his Pineville High School baseball cap.

"Is this your brother?"

Sara has a brother who is a senior at Pineville High

School. I waited for her to introduce us, like how Hope had introduced me to Heath.

"Allegedly," Sara replied, checking the messages on her cell phone.

"Unfortunately," Sara's brother replied.

She did not introduce us. And neither did he.

"Hope's meeting us at the mall," Sara said instead, not looking up from her phone.

Whew. What a relief. I'd never hung out with Sara all by myself before, and I wasn't sure if I could handle being the sole target of her intensity.

"What about Scout?" I asked.

"DON'T EVEN GET ME STARTED ON SCOUT."

"Whoops," Sara's brother muttered under his breath. "Shoulda warned you...."

"You know what she told me? She's wearing her uniform on dance day. HER UNIFORM. That completely wrecks the color scheme for our square...."

"Color scheme?" I asked.

"Of course we have a color scheme!" Sara said. "We want to win, don't we?"

You want to win, I thought, but I knew better than to say it.

"Sara," I began tentatively. "I've only got eleven dollars. I don't think I can afford your color scheme."

"Omigod! Duh! Daddy's Amex!"

And before I could even begin to argue, Sara's brother—named Joe I think?—pulled up to the entrance of Ocean County Mall.

"Grab the returns." Sara gestured toward the Chic Boutique bags stacked next to me. She turned to her brother. "Be back here at four o'clock *sharp*."

"Yes, your majesty," Sara's brother said, barely waiting for us to get to the curb before peeling out of the parking lot.

"Four o'clock? That's six hours from now!"

"Actually, that's five hours and thirty-eight minutes from now," Sara corrected. "Because *someone* couldn't get out of bed and threw off my whole schedule."

With Daddy's credit card in hand, Sara was literally and figuratively ready to take charge. To make up for lost time, she powered her way through the front doors, zooming past a pack of tracksuited senior-citizen mall walkers. I'm a fast runner, but I struggled to keep up because I was weighed down by four Chic Boutique shopping bags.

"Is your brother always so, um…" I searched for the right word. "Slavish?"

"He is when I have major dirt on him that he doesn't want my parents to find out about," she said. "Which I totally do."

I imagined a teenage man like him could get himself into all sorts of trouble.

"Ooh." I was intrigued. "What did you catch him doing?"

Sara came to a sudden stop. She pressed her hands on my shoulders and got all intense and Mr. Wall–like.

"My brother is off topic! Get your act together! Focus! We only have five hours and thirty-six and a half minutes left to shop."

I doubt I've shopped for five hours and thirty-six and a half minutes in my entire life, let alone in one day. Sara relaxed her grip.

"Omigod! Are you ready to shop till you drop?"

"I'd have to actually wake up first before I'd be capable of dropping," I said. "I'm still seventy-five percent asleep."

Sara stopped again.

"I don't think you heard me," she said, barely containing her frustration. "ARE YOU READY TO SHOP TILL YOU DROP?"

There was only one acceptable answer.

"Yes," I replied. "I am ready to shop till I drop."

"Excellent. Because we have arrived."

She swept her arm in front of the Chic Boutique window display of featureless mannequins who were attending a formal dance that looked a lot like Sara's original description of the Glamarama Gala: black-and-white dress code, floor-length formals, tuxedos, crystal accents, orchids and roses and lilies, and that silver carpet—not red carpet, because red can be so harsh in photos...

Sara pointed to the mannequin right in the center of the crowd. It was decked out in a shiny black-and-white polka-dot dress that poufed out at the bottom. More important, it wore a homecoming-queen sash and crown.

"My dream dress!" she squealed. "You make the returns while I scope the store to find dresses that will go with it. It's the best use of both of our time."

She handed me Daddy's Amex and nudged me toward the register.

"How many dresses do you need to buy?" I asked.

"Omigod! For all of us in the square."

Wait. What? Whoa.

"You're buying dresses for the whole square?" I asked.

"Yes! Even Scout! Because there's no way she's getting away with wearing her uniform. Why do you think I'm so stressed?"

Curious, I opened one of the shopping bags and pulled out a dress that looked like it fit me, and I mean that in every way. Like, it suited my figure AND my personality because it was basically a greenish-blue T-shirt but longer. Sara had done a better job shopping for me than I ever could have done for myself. Then again, this shouldn't be such a surprise. She is a professional spender.

"Why are you returning these?"

I held up a long, flowy dress in the same greenish-blue color. It looked perfect for Hope.

"Because they just won't work anymore, that's why," Sara snapped.

"But they're cute and they all match."

If Sara had had Mr. Wall's whistle, she would have blown it right in my face.

"LOOK HERE, SLEEPYHEAD. We're down to five hours and twenty-eight minutes, and I've got the practically impossible task of finding flattering outfits for all of us. Do you have any idea how hard it is to find a dress for Hope that won't come up too short on her or clash with her hair? Or anything that gives some sort of shape to your..." She vaguely gestured in my general direction, as if there were no words to describe the absence of shape that is my body. "You do your job and I'll do mine. So make! Those! Returns!"

Sara took off and immediately started pulling black-and-white dresses off the racks. A salesgirl scurried behind her, struggling to keep up.

I timidly approached the register. Where was Hope when I needed her?

"I'm…um…"

I didn't know how to go about returning hundreds of dollars of clothes, including a dress more expensive than the contents of my entire closet that I hadn't even known Sara had bought for me until she'd ordered me to send it back. Thankfully, this was business as usual for the salesgirl behind the counter.

"Welcome to Chic Boutique I'm Kirsten are you making returns for Miss D'Abruzzi."

She said it just like that. Without punctuation. Without feeling.

"Um…yes."

"My pleasure Miss D'Abruzzi is a valued Chic Boutique client I'll just need the items and do you have the credit card used to make the purchases."

It took me a second to hand it over because I hadn't realized she had asked me a question. Kirsten's teeth were sort of smiling, but her eyes were not. Otherwise, she looked like she'd stepped right out of a Chic Boutique catalog. Everyone who worked at the store did, even the poor girl chasing Sara. They all looked a lot like my sister, who, not coincidentally, works at a different Chic Boutique closer to her school.

Sara rushed up to me clutching the homecoming queen's dress to her heart.

"Omigod! Omigod! Omigod! They have it!" she gushed. "In my size!"

Kirsten smiled at Sara so hard her teeth looked like they were about to crumble down to the nubs.

"You know," she said. "We can always special order anything in"—her eyes narrowed—"*your size.*"

It was the first time Kirsten's voice revealed any trace of human emotion. And that emotion was MEAN. Sara shops here often, so this salesgirl must know she's supersensitive about her size. It's why she eats carrots and celery at lunch every day. She's not fat, but she's not shaped like the Chic Boutique girls, either. She's sort of squarish, I guess, but she wears her clothes well. I mean, Sara is by far the best-dressed girl in school. I worried about how she'd react to the rude salesgirl, but there was no need. I should've assumed Sara has what it takes to handle herself in any tough retail situation.

"I'll remember to do that," Sara said in her sweetest voice, "when you're not here to get the ten percent commission."

ZING! KA-CHING! And OFF SHE WENT.

Unfortunately, I couldn't follow. I had one more return to get through. The first three dresses had gone just fine. The fourth and final dress, however, was a problem.

"We can't take this back not even for store credit I apologize for any inconvenience this may cause you."

She was back to her automated voice. She didn't sound sorry or not sorry. She didn't sound like anything.

"Um, why not?" I asked, wishing Sara would come back to deal with this.

"It's damaged goods the zipper is broken and all the tags have been removed."

Sure enough, she was right. The side zipper had been torn away from the fabric.

"Hey, Sara," I called out tentatively. "I'm having a little bit of a situation over here."

Sara shouted to me from the dressing room at the opposite end of the store.

"AND I'M HAVING A HUGE OMIGOD SITUATION OVER *HERE*. COME! QUICK!"

I bashfully placed the unreturnable dress in the shopping bag, retreated from the register, and took off for the dressing room. Guess who was there wearing Sara's perfect dress? Hint: It wasn't Sara.

"Take it off!" Sara shouted at Manda.

"No way!" Manda shouted at Sara.

"You're not even going to the Down-Home Harvest Dance!" Sara protested. "You don't need it!"

"Puh-leeze. Like your stupid hoedown is the only reason to buy a new dress."

Sara spun around to redirect her anger at Hope, who

was standing off to the side but had little chance of hiding because of her height and hair and all the mirrors.

"And *you*," Sara seethed, "are a traitor to the square for even coming in here with her! You were supposed to shop with me!"

"She just dragged me into the dressing room when she saw me!" Hope said in defense. "I was practically kidnapped."

I gave Hope a sympathetic look that said "Me too." Hope responded with that familiar look of hers, the one that said "We are smarter than this." And I gave her the look that replied "Well, obviously we are not." And she looked back like "Why do we keep letting this happen to us?" and I looked at her like "I honestly don't know," and I swear Hope and I can have entire conversations without ever saying a word out loud. This is a convenient skill to have when many of our conversations are about girls who are standing right in front of us screaming at each other.

"Girls! This is not Chic Boutique behavior!"

This come-to-your-senses moment was brought to us by Bridget, who had entered the dressing room at some point during my telepathic conversation with Hope.

"Bridget? What are you doing here?" I asked.

"I work here," she said proudly.

"You work here?" I asked. "You're twelve."

"Well, not work exactly." She giggled nervously. "It's an educational junior training program."

"Educational junior training program?" Hope asked.

"Yes! Kirsten saw me shopping and stopped me and said I have Chic Boutique potential and that qualifies me for this highly selective educational junior training program that allows me to observe from the inside how Chic Boutique is managed."

Manda, Sara, Hope, and I had the same response.

"What?!?"

Bridget smoothed out invisible wrinkles in her one-shouldered pink-sequined top.

"They give me Chic Boutique clothes, and I wear them."

"That's it?" I asked.

"Pretty much," she replied.

Emphasis on *pretty*. Bridget was recruited by Chic Boutique because she looks like someone who would work at Chic Boutique when she's actually old enough to work at Chic Boutique. Like Kirsten. Like the blonde following Sara around the store. Like my sister.

"Omigod! I spend thousands of dollars in this store, and they give you clothes for free! It's not fair!"

And before Sara could get Daddy's lawyer on it, Manda restored order to the room. Or rather, disorder.

"Attention!" *[clap clap]* "Attention!"

All eyes returned to Manda in Sara's perfect dress.

"I'd like to discuss with Bridget how she might use her educational-junior-training-program discount to get this dress for me."

"I don't think I can do that," Bridget said. "I mean, like, all the clothes I get are in a certain size, and—"

"What's that supposed to mean?" Manda snapped. "Are you saying my dress is the wrong size?"

Well, yeah. That's exactly what Bridget was saying. Manda's dress was the wrong size *for Bridget*. She didn't mean anything bad by it; she was just speaking the truth that we all could see with our own eyes. Bridget is at least three inches taller. And Manda more than makes up for those inches...elsewhere.

"*My* dress," Sara said. "And I don't need a discount to buy it."

"*Your* dress? I don't see your name on it," Manda said mockingly. "And the zipper is still intact and the seams haven't split, so it can't be yours."

Manda of all people should know how sensitive Sara is about her body. Sure, Sara had handled Kirsten's comment without resorting to violence, but I was ready for her to go all-out nuclear now. But she stunned me—and everyone in that tiny dressing room—by keeping her cool.

"Bridget, sweetie?"

"Y-y-yes?" Bridget, too, was petrified.

"Please tell Kirsten that I will purchase this dress…"

"Don't you want to try it on?" she asked.

"Please let me finish," Sara said. "I will purchase this dress in every size you have in stock, including"—she gestured toward Manda without actually looking at her—"*that* one."

"Puh-leeze. You can't do that!"

"Omigod. I totally can."

"Bridget! Can she do that?"

"Yes? No! Maybe? I don't know! This wasn't covered in the educational-junior-training-program pamphlet!"

Bridget ran out of the dressing room to get help from Kirsten, leaving Hope and me alone to keep these BFFs from killing each other.

"This is just one store in one mall in a huge universe of fashion," Hope said, bravely stepping between them. "So let's compromise."

The fact that Manda and Sara had stopped fighting long enough to listen to her says so much about what a powerful, peacemaking presence Hope has been in their lives. Without Hope around, these two surely would have murdered each other by now. In her calmest, most reasonable voice, Hope offered a solution.

"No one gets the dress."

And Manda and Sara responded as I pretty much knew they would.

"I GET THE DRESS!"

They said it at the same time. And I swear they both flinched as they fought the instinct to high-five and shout "Bee-Eff-Effs!"

Hope gave me a look that said "Worst Best Friends Forever Ever," and I had to stifle a laugh. Just when I thought it couldn't get any more dramatic, it did: Sara raised her hand and "zeroed" her WBFFE.

"Oh yeah? Right back at you!" Manda hissed, copying the gesture. "It's the closest you'll ever get to fitting into a size zero!"

"Omigod! Your boobs are totally hanging out! That dress is mine!"

"Puh-leeze. You couldn't even get it over those linebacker shoulders of yours! This dress is mine!"

"Let's hide in the food court," Hope whispered in my ear, "until my parents rescue us."

Together, we quietly tiptoed backward out of the dressing room. As we exited Chic Boutique, Hope led the way, and I trusted her to get me out of there in one piece.

Chapter Nineteen

We took refuge at Cinnabon.

"I think we're safe here," I said.

I was about to add something about how Manda and Sara would come to Cinnabon only if celery sticks were on the menu. But I stopped myself because it sounded like something that snotty salesgirl Kirsten would say, and I didn't want to contribute to all the bad mojo. Manda and Sara fight all the time—it's what they do—but body bashing was a new low. And to be totally honest, I hadn't liked it one bit when Sara complained about how hard it was to shop for our "practically impossible" figures.

Not even gooey baked goods could remove the sour taste all that Chic Boutique drama had left in my mouth. I might as well have been gnawing on one of my mother's nasty Tofurky balls. I set my Cinnabon down on a napkin and pushed it away from me. This got Hope's attention, as I'm not known for passing up sweets.

"Have they always been so terrible to each other?" I asked.

Hope chewed for a few seconds before answering.

"They've always been competitive, but it used to be in a more positive way. Who got the higher score on a math test, that sort of thing."

"Really?"

The same girls who shout "Nerd alert!" whenever I ace a Pre-Algebra test? I couldn't imagine them once competing for high math scores.

"Oh yeah! Or, like, in second grade, Manda got it in her head that she wanted to win the geography bee, which pushed Sara to memorize every state capital."

"Who won?" I asked.

Hope smiled shyly. "I did."

My heart did a little victory dance at the idea of Hope beating Manda and Sara in a second-grade geography bee.

"Anyway, they used to push each other to do better. Even the comPETITION wasn't all bad, because they had a common goal, right? But now they're trying to outdo each other in totally useless ways, like who looks better in a dumb dress or whatever. And it's getting way worse." Hope licked frosting off her thumb. "I'm starting to wonder whether Manda's doctor is right. Maybe her hormones are to blame."

"But *you* have hormones, and I *supposedly* have hormones, and we're not acting like them," I said. "*Everyone* has hormones, and *no one* acts like they do."

"No one that we know of. But I'm sure there are Mandas and Saras outside of the G and T classes, or in eighth grade. Definitely at other schools." She paused to slurp a mouthful of soda. "I bet there have been Mandas and Saras all throughout history."

I thought of Bethany's nonadvice about stressing, obsessing, and second-guessing. IT List 3 didn't come right out and say *Hey, here's help with the perils of pubertizing*, because my sister was savvy about public relations even back then and ew, who would want to read an IT List all about *that*? But that's what all her *don't compare* and *early, late*, and *middle bloomer* business was about, wasn't it? My sister must have suffered through the hormonal freak-outs of girls like Manda and Sara. Or, even more likely, she might have been one of those girls herself. IT List #5: No one knows anything.

"I wish there was a way to get them to make peace by working together again," Hope said, balling up a napkin and tossing it on our table. "If only Manda wanted to win the Hoedown Showdown as much as Sara."

"She couldn't care less about it," I pointed out.

"Now," Hope said, looking off into the distance like she

was concentrating on something. "But maybe we could get her to care somehow..."

She didn't finish her thought, because a commotion was headed straight for us at top speed on his skateboard.

A commotion named Heath.

"What's wrong? Is everything okay?" He was all out of breath. "I left as soon as I got your message!"

"What are you doing here?" Hope asked. "And why aren't you wearing your helmet?"

"I'm here to rescue you!" Heath said, still panting. "To bring you home."

"On your skateboard?" I asked.

There was definitely not enough room for three of us on his skateboard.

"No," he said, lowering his voice. "In the car."

"You drove the car?!"

"Shhhhhhh..."

He clamped his hands over Hope's mouth.

"Look, Mom and Dad are always stressing, like, if you're ever in a sketchy situation and need help, don't hesitate to call day or night and we'll come get you...."

Hope escaped her brother's clutches.

"*They'll* come get me! Not you! You don't even have a license."

"I've got my permit," Heath said. "Which is practically the same thing."

"It's logic like that," Hope said through gritted teeth, "that keeps you grounded for life."

I tried to break the tension with a joke.

"So who do we call to rescue us from our rescuer?"

Hope wasn't in a joking mood. She slapped her brother on the forehead.

"OW!"

"If you were wearing a helmet, that wouldn't have hurt."

This was superawkward. I decided to let the siblings work it out on their own.

"I'm just gonna..."

I thumbed in the direction of the restrooms. I doubt Hope or Heath even noticed as I slunk away.

"Do you realize the position you've put me in? I have to tell Mom and Dad you took the car...."

"To rescue you!"

They were still going at it when I rounded the bend and—WHOOPS!—came thisclose to running right into the middle of a conversation between Scotty and Burke. Ack. Was everyone at Ocean County Mall this morning?

"We're better on defense," Burke was saying.

"Yeah, but we can't win if we don't score," Scotty was saying.

I'd put in way too much time with Scotty in gym class this week. Today was my day off. Fortunately they were too distracted by game talk to spot me as I ducked and took cover behind a nearby soda machine.

"I can't believe Coach threatened to bench us if we don't go to this stupid dance," Burke said.

"It's the only way to get any guys to go," Scotty said.

That wasn't true. I'm pretty sure no one is *forcing* Aleck to attend.

"Your girl is happy," Scotty continued, referring to Bridget.

"Winning the Hoedown Showdown is all she talks about," Burke said. "Is Dori still giving you crap about not dancing with her?"

"It's not like I had a choice," Scotty said. "If Dori were in my gym class, I would've picked her. But she's not. So I didn't."

I should have left at that moment. But nooooo. I just had to stick around and listen. Sara deserves some credit. Eavesdropping isn't as easy as it looks.

"Who's your partner again?" Burke asked.

"This girl Jessica," Scotty replied offhandedly. "She's in my classes."

The hairs on the back of my neck stood up.

"Nerd classes," Burke replied.

"Shut up," Scotty said. This was followed by sounds of grunts and shoving.

"Which one's Jessica?" Burke asked. "Is she the one with the big... heart?"

Both boys grunt-laughed like *huhuhuhuhuhuh*.

"Nah," Scotty said. "That's Manda."

Riiiight. Manda needs extra underwire support for her big *heart*.

"The loud one?"

Two sets of sneakers came closer, followed by the sounds of coins sliding into the machine.

"OMIGOD!!!" Scotty shouted. "That's Sara."

The imitation made Burke laugh out loud. I might have laughed, too, if I'd allowed myself to breathe.

"The tall one with the red hair?"

I pressed myself against the wall as if I could change into gray cinder-block camouflage like a chameleon. I hoped the boys were too focused on choosing caffeinated beverages to notice the subject of their conversation was HOLDING HER BREATH SIX INCHES AWAY.

"Nope," Scotty said. "Hope."

There was a pause followed by the *ka-chunk* sound of a soda being dispensed.

"I don't know who this Jessica girl is," Burke said.

Really, Burke? Really?!?

YOU KNOW WHO I AM. I RIDE THE BUS WITH YOU EVERY SINGLE DAY. I LIVE ACROSS THE STREET FROM YOUR GIRLFRIEND AND WAS HER BEST FRIEND UNTIL YOU STOLE HER AWAY FROM ME.

"You know who she is," Scotty said. "She rides the bus with you. She lives across from Bridget. They were best friends until..."

GO ON. TELL HIM, SCOTTY. WE WERE BEST FRIENDS UNTIL YOU STOLE HER AWAY FROM ME.

"Oh yeah," Burke butted in. "The smart one?"

The smart one?

"Yes! The smart one," Scotty replied.

Huh, I thought. *I'm the smart one.*

Fortunately, I liked being known as the smart one.

Unfortunately, I wasn't smart enough to quit while I was ahead.

"Bridget says she's a real brainiac," Burke said.

The sneakers were joined by a third set of feet, in pink sheepskin boots.

"Who's a real brainiac?" Dori asked.

SERIOUSLY. WAS EVERYONE AT OCEAN COUNTY MALL THIS MORNING?

"Your boyfriend's square-dance partner," Burke replied. "She's freakishly smart."

"Well," Dori struck back, "she may be abnormally ahead in the brain, but she's abnormally behind in the bra."

Both boys grunt-laughed like *huhuhuhuhuhuh.*

"She's built like a first grader," Burke joked.

"It's true!" Dori added. "And I should know because I've known her since elementary school!"

This is what I got for eavesdropping. It's one thing to have a negative opinion about yourself when you're having a bad day or whatever. But it's an entirely different thing when you hear your worst thoughts spoken aloud by someone else.

"Dori, I can't believe you ever thought Scotty had a thing for that girl," Burke said.

"I know, right?"

And then I heard gross kissy-kissy sounds.

"Know why Jessica's called the Woodchick?" Scotty asked.

The Woodchick? *Who calls me the Woodchick?*

"Why is she called the Woodchick?" Dori replied.

Hmm... because I'm the only girl in Woodshop?

"Because she's the only girl in Woodshop," he said. "And..."

Aaaaaand?

"She's flat as a board!"

Scotty, Dori, and Burke laughed like my humiliation was the most hilarious thing that had ever happened in the history of Ocean County Mall.

I know I should have been relieved to hear that Scotty didn't think of me as girlfriend material anymore. Ha! I'd proven I'm not crushable after all! But that didn't mean I had to stand there with my back pressed up against the wall and listen to the three of them mock me because I'm

163

not pubertizing yet. I leaped out from behind the soda machine to confront them.

"YOU!" I thrust my finger at Scotty. "And YOU." At Burke. "And YOU." At Dori.

The three of them jumped backward like I was a hobgoblin about to steal their souls. It's a good thing I had the element of surprise going for me, because as smart as I am, I didn't have anything clever to say.

"YOU ARE MEAN."

It wasn't my finest moment. Definitely not my best comeback. But it was far better than not saying anything at all.

I'd retreated halfway through the food court before I realized I didn't have anywhere safe to go. I hadn't looked back to see if Scotty, Burke, and Dori were following me, but I wasn't about to slow down to find out. Hope was still at the table where I'd left her, but Heath was nowhere to be seen. I shot her a look that said "Come with me," and she raised her eyebrow to say "Why?" and when I sped past her without slowing down to answer or wipe away my tears, she got up and followed. She didn't know where I was going or why I was in such a hurry to get there. My silent request was clear: I needed her.

And that was all Hope needed to know.

Chapter Twenty

I estimated the ten-minute car ride would take me about ninety minutes on foot. If I were by myself, that is. I appreciated Hope's company, but she was wearing these clogs that were apparently very comfortable but not built for speed. She slowed our pace considerably, which would've been okay, I guess, if the weather had been cooperating.

"So what happened?" Hope asked, looking up at the clouds glooming in the sky.

I opened my mouth to tell her what Scotty and Dori and Burke had said about me, but I got choked up all over again before I could get the words out. Ugh. It made no sense. I don't even like any of them. Why did their opinions matter so much to me, anyway? I almost prayed for a downpour so I could blame my tears on the rain. Hope must have realized that I was in no condition to talk just yet. So she told me what happened with Heath.

"I sent him home," she said, "and I promised I wouldn't tell our parents that he'd taken their car, which puts me in an awkward position because they should know what he did, but I don't want Heath to get in trouble, because his heart is always in the right place even if his brain is stuck somewhere else."

We'd just gotten to the on/off ramp that connects the parking lot to the main road. A long, wet trudge was still ahead of us.

"Oh, and another thing," Hope said. "I got a message from Sara while you were in the bathroom. We're dismissed from her square."

That was the best news I'd heard this whole rotten day. No square = no square dancing = no Down-Home Harvest Dance = no Hoedown Showdown. I'd rather lose a limb in Woodshop than hold Scotty's jerky hand ever again.

"And Manda's agreed to take your spot, so I guess we got what we wished for, huh? The Worst Best Friends Forever Ever together ag—"

Hope stopped midsentence and suddenly picked up the pace.

"Don't look back," she said nervously, "but I think we're being followed."

As soon as she said it, I got the "uh-oh" feeling. Hope and I were about to become the cautionary tale for a bazillion STRANGER-DANGER assemblies. Our school photos would serve as sad reminders of what happens when defenseless youngsters go around unsupervised....

A car horn honked, and Hope and I almost leaped into each other's arms.

"Jessie!"

I made a move to look, and Hope tried to stop me.

"Keep walking!" she urged.

"Jessie!"

I've known that voice my entire life.

"Jessie! Where are you going?"

Sure enough, I turned around to see my sister leaning out of the driver's side of her latest boyfriend's borrowed car.

"What are you doing here?" Bethany asked.

"I was about to ask you the same thing," I said.

My sister does not waste her time or money at Ocean County Mall. Not when there are *numerous superior shopportunities between here and school.*

"I was called in as a Chic Boutique crisis counselor." She said it straight-faced and as serious as could be. "There was a major incident at the store."

Hope and I exchanged looks: Manda and Sara!

"And the useless assistant manager called me for backup."

Hope and I exchanged more looks: Kirsten!

"As much as Chic Boutique needs me right now, I'd be bailing on my big-sisterly duties if I let you and your friend…"

"Hope," she helpfully replied. "We met once before."

"I remember the hair," my sister said, "just not the name."

Hope's lips puckered slightly, but she didn't say anything.

"Anyway, I'm not letting you and Hope walk home in the rain," my sister said, unlocking the car doors. "Get in."

It was really coming down now, so we got in the backseat without an argument. I'd barely gotten my seat belt on before the grilling began.

"So what happened?" Hope asked.

"Something happened?" Bethany asked.

"Nothing," I said, trying not to get all worked up again. "Nothing happened."

Bethany and Hope released disappointed sighs.

"Seriously," I insisted. "Everything's fine."

No one spoke. The windshield wipers filled the silence with a *wish-wish-wishing* sound. I couldn't take it anymore.

"I wish I weren't such a freak!" I blurted.

"You are not a freak," Bethany replied quickly. "Darlings aren't freaks."

It was clear Bethany refused to acknowledge any possible freakishness in our shared bloodline.

"Fine, I'm not a freak," I said. "But I'm not normal, either."

"Who's normal?" Hope asked.

"Manda and Sara are normal."

Hope shuddered. "You want to be like Manda and Sara?"

"No!" I said. "But I think it would be easier if I were."

"Why do you think that?" my sister asked.

"You're normal," I said. "And junior high was a breeze for you."

To my sister's credit, Most Popular, Prettiest, Miss Perfect didn't try to argue.

"I don't want to be normal," Hope said. "Normal is boring." Then to my sister, "Um, no offense!"

"None taken," Bethany said. "Where is this all coming from? This isn't about the IT List, is it? Or the Crushability Quiz?"

"No!" I insisted. "And no!"

"The *what* list?" asked Hope. "The *what* quiz?"

"Nothing," I said, shooting my sister a look in the rearview mirror. "And nothing."

Hope slumped in her seat and sucked disapprovingly on her teeth.

"Nothing," I repeated lamely.

Hope bolted upright and flashed hand signs in front of my face.

"Did you just '*zero*' me?" I asked.

"I did," Hope said, as if she were challenging me. "Because there's a whole lot of nothing going on with you today."

My sister gave an "Aha!" of approval from the front seat.

I deserved the zeroes. Hope deserved better. And I guess my sister did, too.

So I told them what I'd heard when I was hiding behind the soda machine. And they got appropriately offended on my behalf.

"SHE DID NOT SAY THAT."

"She did."

"HE DID NOT SAY THAT."

"He did."

"THEY DID NOT SAY THAT."

"They did."

By the time we got to my house, I was feeling better, but not okay, about what had happened at the mall. It was good to get it all out, I guess, even if talking didn't change anything. I'm still the Woodchick. Flat as a board. Or a first grader.

It had stopped raining, and as we got out of the car, the reemerging sunlight hit Hope's hair just so.

"Your hair is the most amazing shade," my sister marveled.

Hope looked around with legit "Who, me?" cluelessness.

"I must know," my sister pressed. "Is it your natural color?"

"Of course it is!" Hope replied. "Why would anyone willingly dye their hair the same color as Cheetos?"

My sister shook her head and sighed.

"Hope, your hair is the color of a tropical bird-of-paradise flower."

Hope doesn't fluster easily, but my sister's compliment caught her totally off guard.

"Um. Gee. Thanks. Um."

"And while we're at it, Jessie, your flat-as-a-boardness, those long limbs, and that narrow waist is, like, the ideal body type in South Korea."

"So you're saying I should move to South Korea...?"

My sister hushed me up with a finger snap.

"I'm saying you both see yourselves all wrong," she said. "You're in transition! You'll never be who you once were, but you're still turning into who you will be. It's an exciting time! Embrace it!"

Aha! So that's what Bethany meant by IT List #3: Be a middle bloomer!

A flash of insight must have crossed my face because Bethany paused just long enough to smile at me. It wasn't one of her attention-getting dazzlers, but a quiet upturn of the lips that's rarer and more prized.

"And another thing," my sister continued. "Hope is right about normal. It's boring."

She beckoned us to come closer, as if she were letting us in on something even more confidential than the Top Secret Pineville Junior High Crushability Quiz.

"That's why I'm going to teach you how to fly the coop!"

"What the what?" Hope and I asked.

"Fly the coop," she repeated. "You don't know how to fly the coop?"

Unless she was referring to one of my infamous Mighty the Seagull dance moves, I had no idea what she was talking about.

"I shouldn't be surprised you've never heard of it," she said. "It's a top secret square-dance strategy."

Hope and I burst out laughing.

"Top secret square-dance strategy?" I asked. "There's no strategy in square dancing. You just do what the caller tells you to do."

"That's where you're wrong, Jessie," Bethany said

knowingly. "My sorority flew the coop and won the Greek Week Do-Si-Do Rodeo when I was a sophomore. You said the dance is Friday, right?"

We nodded.

"If you can master this maneuver, your square is guaranteed to win the Hoedown Showdown."

"But we don't have a square anymore," I said. "We've been dismissed."

"You've got me and Mike," Hope said. "And I know we can get the Scouts on board, too, because they don't respect Sara's leadership style."

Even if the Scouts, Hope, and Basketball Mike joined me, that still left us one couple short of a square. Not to mention the fact that I kind of hated my partner at the moment. Neither of these details seemed to trouble my sister one bit.

"Technically, only two out of the eight in your square are allowed to know you're flying the coop," my sister explained. "Usually it's a dancer and a partner, but it doesn't have to be. You two will do just fine. So. Do you want me to teach it to you or not?"

I usually don't like agreeing to things before I know what it is I'm agreeing to. But Hope looked pretty enthusiastic about flying the coop, so I decided to follow her open-minded example.

"Just promise not to yell at us like you do to the girls on your sorority dance team," I said. "I'm tired of all the yelling."

My sister promised. And I chose to believe her.

"All right. Let's do it," I said. "Let's fly the coop."

Whatever that meant.

Unfortunately, I was no closer to getting it even after my sister's half-hour lecture/lesson on the topic.

"If your square is truly working together," Bethany said after she had shown us sample choreography, "you can do your own thing but, like, as a team."

Hope nodded, so I did, too.

"*That's* flying the coop."

I'd started to wonder whether all my sister's wisdom was lost without the yelling. Apparently not, because Hope, free spirit that she is, caught on to the concept much faster than I did.

"Spontaneous synchronization!"

Bethany beamed at her star student. "Exactly!"

They both looked eagerly at me. I felt compelled to prove I also understood.

"Um," I said. "Synchronized spontaneity!"

This must have been the right answer because the next thing I knew all three of us were tangled up in a group hug.

"You can't lose!" Bethany insisted as she waved good-bye to us.

"We can't lose!" Hope said excitedly as we waved good-bye to Bethany.

They were confident we could pull it off. I agreed only in an attempt to match their level of enthusiasm.

"We can't lose?"

I wasn't very convincing.

"We can do this," Hope said encouragingly. "Think about everything we manage to say to each other without saying a word."

"But that's between you and me," I said. "What if no one else in our square catches on and we just look like two crazy people?"

Hope was thoroughly untroubled by this possibility.

"The hardest part," Hope continued, "will be keeping quiet about it until Friday night!"

Um, not so hard for me, because I had no idea how to explain what it was we had supposedly just learned.

Hope swung her leg over my dad's old bike she'd borrowed for the ride home. Even after adjusting the seat to its maximum height, my ten-speed had been too small for her. She'd looked like she was squeezing herself behind the handlebars of a toddler's tricycle. Hope was, after all, the height of a full-grown man. And yet she carried herself without any of the gangliness usually associated with girls who are tall beyond their years.

I guess I was looking at her in a funny way she couldn't translate.

"What?" she asked.

"I was just thinking how cool it would be to be so tall and graceful like you."

Hope nearly fell off the bike. This would've been okay because she'd already strapped on a helmet.

"Are you kidding?"

"No," I replied. "I'm not kidding."

"You wouldn't say that if you knew what it was like to look at the tops of heads all day long! And my neck hurts! I'm twelve years old, and I need a chiropractor because I'm constantly looking down at everyone!"

I didn't know this.

"I bet you envy Manda's boobs, don't you? Well, she's got back pain even worse than I do! No wonder she's so cranky. And you know why Sara is such a shopaholic? It's because she keeps outgrowing her clothes!"

I thought about Manda's mood swings and the broken zipper on Sara's Chic Boutique dress. Hope's observations made sense. I'd just never bothered to pay attention.

"And who cares if Scotty thinks you're flat as a board! You wouldn't be the awesome runner you are if you were built like anyone else."

It's true. I haven't come across too many top-heavy distance runners.

Hope was shaking her head at me disappointedly. She and I were really getting somewhere friendshipwise. I couldn't handle the thought that I'd blown it all with one stupid comment I'd meant as a compliment.

"Are you mad at me?" I asked.

"Of course not!" she said, laughing. "I'm just tired of everyone complaining about their appearance. It's the Salvador Dalí in me, maybe. Normal is boring. I see beauty in oddity."

She pushed the kickstand with her foot.

"We need to be more realistic about everyone else's so-called advantages and more forgiving about our so-called shortcomings."

"Or, *tall*comings," I said, "in your case."

Thankfully, Hope laughed at my joke, so I laughed, too.

"You should listen to your sister," Hope said as she pedaled down the driveway. "We're in midbloom. Let's embrace it!"

Hope had given me the perfect opportunity to tell her what happens whenever I attempt to follow my sister's advice. But by the time I was ready to confess the truth about the IT Lists and the Crushability Quiz, she'd already pedaled too far down the road. Another time, I promised myself. Another time.

I'd just turned to go back inside the house when I heard a voice.

"Jess!"

Scotty. Ack. What was he doing here? And how had he gotten here without passing Hope? I was torn between taking off and telling him off. His hand was on my shoulder before I could decide.

"I thought Hope would never leave," he said.

I shook him off but refused to face him.

"You eavesdropped on our conversation? Creeper!"

"Isn't that what you did to me? Why were you lurking behind the soda machine?"

"That was an accident. Wrong place at the wrong time. You intentionally hid in the bushes to listen to me and Hope. There's a huge difference!"

"I wasn't listening; I was waiting to talk to you alone," Scotty said, sneaking around me so I'd have to look at him. "You weren't supposed to hear any of those things I said at the mall."

"Obviously," I snapped. "That's the whole point of talking behind someone's back, isn't it?"

And I turned away from him again just to make my point.

"I had to say those things in front of Dori!" he claimed. "She's jealous that we're partners and—"

"*Were* partners," I corrected him. "Because you're crazy if you think I'm dancing with you after getting insulted like that."

"But, Jess—"

"But nothing," I said. "I'm sure you'll find a suitable replacement for me in the Woodshop supply closet. There are plenty of flat-as-a-board two-by-fours to choose from."

I slammed the front door in Scotty's face and congratulated myself on a comeback worthy of someone as smart as everyone thinks I am. The celebration was short-lived, however, because a moment later it hit me: I didn't have a partner.

Without a partner, our square was incomplete.

And an incomplete square can't fly the coop.

Chapter Twenty-One

Bridget couldn't wait for me to show up at the bus stop Monday morning. She actually rang my doorbell while I was in the bathroom brushing my teeth. This delighted my mother to no end. She's missed Bridget more than ever since she turned pretty.

"Bridget! How lovely to see you! Are you excited about Friday night? I'm sure Jessie has told you that we'll be there at the Down-Home Harvest Dance!"

I hadn't told Bridget any such thing, because I was still hoping for an act of divine parental intervention that would prevent my parents from fulfilling their chaperoning duties.

"How could you leave me alone in the middle of all that drama?" Bridget asked when I came down the stairs.

"You weren't alone," I pointed out as I put on my jacket. "You had Kirsten as backup."

"What drama?" my mother asked eagerly, plopping herself down on the bottom step like it was story time at the library.

"There was a fight over a dress," I replied as I shouldered my backpack.

My mother jerked to attention.

"Jessie! You got into a fight? Over a dress?"

I'm not sure what part sounded more incredible to my mother: the fight or the possibility that it was over a dress.

"Oh no! Not me! Manda and Sara!"

"Well, they're Bee-Eff-Effs again," Bridget informed me. "And you're out of the square."

Hope had told me as much, but it was a relief to hear it confirmed from a second source.

"Let me guess. Manda's in?"

"Yeah, and, um, here's the other thing," Bridget said, pulling nervously on a strand of hair by her left ear. "Sara's going to arrange it so Dori replaces you as Scotty's partner, which makes sense. I mean, it's only right that couples get to dance with each other, right?"

"I'm sorry," my mother interrupted. "I'm having trouble keeping up."

Bridget pressed on. But reluctantly.

181

"Well, um, you think you can tell Hope that she's out, too?" she asked timidly. "Because I don't really know her all that well, and it's kind of awkward."

Okay. So Bridget didn't know that Hope was already out. But it still didn't make sense for her to be acting all squirrelly about the changes to the square...

UNTIL IT TOTALLY DID.

"You and Burke are in! You're joining Manda and Sara's Supersquare!"

"I'm sorry, Jess!" Bridget said, genuinely apologetic. "The only way Dori and I could get Burke and Scotty to go to the dance was if we were all together."

I knew this wasn't true. I'd overheard them saying their basketball coach was forcing them to participate. But I didn't say this, because honestly, at this point, I didn't care. I was free from tyrannical Sara, terrifying Manda, and two-faced Scotty. That's all that mattered.

My mother, of course, didn't understand any of this.

"Who are Manda and Sara?" she asked. "And why do they have the power to kick anyone out of anything?"

Bridget and I looked at each other and shrugged. There wasn't a clear, concise answer to either one of those questions. None we could deliver without missing the bus that was already coming down the street.

"Gotta go!"

As Bridget and I ran for the bus, I thought about her boyfriend's participation in my humiliation. If I were dating a jerk, I'd want to know. Even better, I'd like to think I'm savvy enough not to date a jerk in the first place. But the world is full of sneaky jerks, isn't it? Ones who put on their nice faces when they think the important people are watching but who are jerks to everyone else. So when I got on board and saw Burke, all smiles for Bridget in the backseat, I decided it might be more effective if I just talked to him myself. Instead of taking my usual seat, I followed Bridget to the rear.

"Hi, Burke. I'm Jessica. Remember me? We ran into each other by the soda machine at the mall. I'm the Smart One. Smart enough not to let your jerky judgments get me down."

I said it all at once before I lost my nerve.

Bridget looked at me as if I were mad. Which I *thought* I was. As in mad/angry, not mad/crazy. But, after seeing the shaken expression on Burke's face as I confronted him, I wasn't mad anymore.

I was relieved he wasn't my boyfriend.

"What is she talking about?" Bridget asked Burke.

"N-n-nothing," Burke stammered back at Bridget.

"What did you say to her?"

"Nothing!"

Satisfied, I walked back and took my regular seat in the middle of the bus. I'd told the truth. It was up to Bridget to decide what to do with it.

"Make room," Bridget said, sliding next to me into the seat.

She'd decided to side with me. At least for the time being.

"Listen, I don't know what he said to you, and you don't have to tell me. I know his sense of humor can be really..." She held up her hands in surrender. "I'm sorry."

"You have nothing to apologize for."

"I want to apologize on his behalf," she said.

"He should apologize on his own behalf," I said.

One of the back-of-the-bus boys farted. Burke and all the rest laughed like gorillas. *Huhuhuhuhuh.* Bridget stole a quick glance over her shoulder.

"Burke makes jokes that aren't very funny sometimes."

The way she said it made me wonder if Burke had ever made jokes at her expense. And what she said next convinced me of it.

"Sometimes I wonder if Burke would even like me at all if I hadn't gotten..."

Her voice trailed off.

"You can say it, Bridget," I said. "It's okay."

"Say what?"

"Pretty," I supplied for her. "Would he be your boyfriend if you hadn't gotten pretty?"

Bridget's cheeks turned pink.

"Jess! I would never say that about myself!"

I had to agree. Even if she were aware of her own attractiveness—which she has to be, right?—she's far too modest to admit it.

"Would Burke be my boyfriend if I hadn't gotten my braces off?" she asked. "Would he like me if I still had a mouth full of metal?"

"So what you're really asking is," I said, "would he still like you if you weren't pretty?"

She shoved me surprisingly hard against the window. "Stop saying that!"

"But it's true, Bridget! By our culture's standards of beauty, you're pretty. Don't apologize for it. Own it! And, as your boyfriend, Burke should appreciate your big blue eyes and cute little nose and clear skin and blond hair because they're all parts of YOU."

I had Bridget's full attention, but who knew how much longer it would last? The bus was pulling into the parking lot, so I decided to go for it.

"Here's the most important thing: Your looks aren't all of you. So they shouldn't be the only thing he or anyone else appreciates about you."

Bridget smiled and rested her head on my shoulder.

"Thanks, Jess," she said. "I hope you realize how lucky you are to be the Smart One."

And at that moment, I honestly did.

My conversation with Bridget got me thinking about what Hope had said about our imperfections—real and imagined. I mean, I'd never once considered that Bridget's beauty could be anything but an advantage, and that was *before* I knew she's getting free clothes from the coolest store at the mall just because of how good she looks in them. But how would I feel if my (totally imaginary) boyfriend never listened to me because he thought I was too pretty to have anything worth saying?

I wouldn't like that at all.

So for the rest of the day, and the rest of the week, I kept thinking about everyone's bodies.

ACK. THAT CAME OUT ALL WRONG.

Like, I'd assumed all along that Manda contorts herself into those attention-getting poses just to remind everyone of her boobs. But after Hope told me about her back pain, I was willing to consider that she's just trying to stretch out her sore muscles. And I'd thought Sara's addicted to shopping. Maybe I could feel a little bad about how she rarely gets to enjoy any favorite item of clothing before it doesn't fit anymore.

Here's the most important thing I've discovered from all this watching: More than anything else, it's your *attitude* that determines whether what's outside is an accurate reflection of what's inside. And Manda and Sara were ESPECIALLY ANNOYING THIS WEEK. Inside and out.

So as much as I'd wanted to give them the benefit of the doubt, I couldn't. Not when they spent Monday through Friday bragging about how they were destined to win the Hoedown Showdown with their new-and-improved Supersquare: Sara and Sam, Manda and Vinnie, Scotty and Dori, Bridget and Burke.

"I'm sorry, Jess!" Bridget whispered quickly when I passed her in the gym.

She'd made her choice: Burke. And was maybe even legitimately remorseful about it. But I didn't give her the "It's okay" smile she wanted because—guess what?—it wasn't okay. Not when Hope, Basketball Mike, the Scouts, and I were left to scramble to fill in our square with, well, the leftovers. There was runny-nosed John-John, of course, and a mushy-mouthed couple who sit in the back of our G&T classes and never speak above a mumble to anyone but each other. They were, you know, the odd kids out who no one else wanted.

And I can say that because I was one of them.

Every time John-John spun right instead of left, walked

forward instead of back, or accidentally joined the ladies-only chain, Hope would give me a look that said "Don't worry!" or "We've got this!" or "We're gonna fly the coop!"

I gave her only one look in return. It said "My hand is covered in John-John's snot."

Meanwhile, on the other side of the gym, the Super-square asserted their dominance over the rest of us. At this point in our training, Sara had finally turned on the music. They yelped, yeehawed, and yahooed along with the recorded banjos and fiddles. They were the most popular, pretty, and perfect Pineville Junior High had to offer, and they made the impossible possible:

They made square dancing look cool.

The Leftovers definitely did not.

"Secret weapon!" Hope said energetically after today's massive eight-person promenade pileup that finished our final practice session. "We'll still win tonight!"

"Tonight?" John-John asked. "The dance is tonight?"

And that's when John-John informed us that neither he nor the mumblecouple would be joining us at the Down-Home Harvest Dance. Evidently, they have online role-play gaming parties on Friday nights. And there's no way John-John was about to ditch his Canadian computer girlfriend he's never met in person just to lose in the first round of the Hoedown Showdown.

"Sorry," he said, wiping his nose with his hand.

"Srmphrry," said the mumblecouple.

"They're not sorry at all," I said to Hope.

"Nope," she agreed.

The Leftovers had better love lives than we did. Not that I'm, like, desperate for a love life or anything. As if being rejected by John-John wasn't embarrassing enough, Manda really had to rub in the humiliation.

"Vinnie is the dreamiest partner ever!"

She gushed pretty hard for a girl who already had a boyfriend. All week I'd thought it was weird that Manda was dancing with Vinnie instead of Mouth. Sara had gone out of her way to arrange for Bridget and Dori (who conveniently had Mr. Armbruster for Social Studies that period) and Burke (who usually had Study Hall) to switch to our gym class to practice for the dance, and yet, she hadn't done the same for Mouth.

I hadn't talked to him or Aleck or any of the Wood-shop boys all week because we had different decoration duties: They were busy raising the (fake) barn, and I was busy raising the (fake) livestock. Whenever I did catch a glimpse of either of them, they both seemed to be in serious moods. Like, usually Aleck and Mouth joke around while they work. But this week, they simply followed Sara's orders, like there was nothing remotely ironic about gluing thousands of individual rhinestones to a fake pigpen.

I finally caught up with Mouth and Aleck after school on Friday. Since she'd never bothered forming a true committee for the dance, Sara had to bribe volunteers with sodas and snacks to help set up the decorations. The boys were hauling two silver spray-painted bales of hay off a hand truck they'd wheeled from Woodshop to the gym.

"So are you two ready for the dance?" I asked.

Mouth sat down on the hay, put his head in his hands, and moaned.

"You *had* to ask, didn't you?" Aleck said.

"What did I say?" I asked.

"Manda dumped him for her square-dance partner," Aleck said. "Vinnie whatshisname."

Mouth moaned louder.

"Oh no," I said. "I'm so sorry."

I couldn't say I didn't see it coming.

"What about you?" I asked.

"I'm withdrawing from the competition in solidarity," Aleck said. "And also because my partner ditched me."

How could I have forgotten? Dori was Aleck's partner before she was Scotty's!

"That's too bad," I said. "I was really looking forward

to seeing those so-called superior square-dancing skills of yours."

And then a wonderful thing happened. My overthinking brain finally worked to my advantage. Just like that, I had an idea that could solve all our square-dancing problems. (Which, by the way, is a category of problems I could've never imagined having until two weeks ago.)

All I had to do was ask.

Ask.

Just ask.

What was the big deal? We were all friends, right? Just friends. Friends who'd deploy a top secret combination of superior skills and synchronized spontaneity to overthrow the Supersquare once and for all.

If I asked.

So.

I asked.

"What if I told you about a square still missing a few sides?"

And on the strength of their smiles alone, it was decided. Aleck and Mouth had officially joined the Leftovers.

Chapter Twenty-Two

I'd hardly had any time to congratulate myself on this master stroke of brilliance when Sara came charging at us in full freak-out.

"This is a disaster!" Sara screeched. "They're not supposed to be in the gym now!"

"Who?" I asked.

"The wrestling team! They're practicing in the gym this afternoon! Of all afternoons!"

"If I'm not mistaken," Aleck said, "they practice there every afternoon."

Mr. Pudel arrived on the scene to inspect all the decorations before installation.

"My plans!" Sara shrieked at him. "My plans are ruined!"

"Bruiser," Mr. Pudel said calmly, "before drawing up your elaborate plans, did you even check to make sure the gymnasium was free this afternoon?"

"Omigod!" was all Sara could bring herself to say.

"Lucky for you, they'll be finished by four," Mr. Pudel assured her. "Plenty of time to set up."

"See?" I said to Sara. "Nothing to worry about."

"Easy for you to say, with your nonexistent beauty routine," Sara said. "I've got appointments starting at three thirty. Hair! Nails! Exfoliation!"

"We'll be fine without you," Mr. Pudel said.

Sara hesitated.

"Mr. Pudel takes great pride in his work," I insisted, "and will expect nothing less than perfection from his volunteers."

Mr. Pudel nodded. Aleck grinned. Mouth scowled.

"Okay," Sara agreed reluctantly. "But if there's so much as a ... a ... *strand* of hay out of place ..."

And she took off without even bothering to finish the threat.

I was actually pretty excited by this turn of events. I'd wanted to see Molly wrestle ever since I'd heard about her making the team! But we had a lot of work to do first. Just getting all the decorations from one side of the school to the other required many hands and several trips. When we were finally done transporting everything for the dance from the Woodshop to just outside the gym, there were only about ten minutes left in her practice.

Still, that was just enough time to watch Molly beat an eighth-grade boy in a rope-climbing race. She ascended hand over hand to the ceiling like it was the easiest thing in the world! It wasn't the same as a match, of course, but it was still pretty cool to see her more than hold her own with the boys. Aleck, Mouth, and I stopped her on the way to the girls' locker room.

"Molly! You're amazing! You kicked that boy's butt!"

"Thanks," she said shyly, wiping sweat from her brow.

"You flew up that rope faster than I ever could," Aleck admitted.

"Thanks," she said again, looking at her feet.

"Hey, is Coach Wall making your team go to the dance tonight?"

I normally wouldn't have asked Molly about the dance, but I remembered what Scotty and Burke had said about their coach making it mandatory.

"Yeah. I'm supposed to. But my partner from gym class isn't going, because he's got a gaming date with his online girlfriend, so…"

Well, *that* was unexpected. Not *what* Molly said— apparently a lot of kids cuddle up to their game controllers on Friday nights—but *how* she said it. She sounded disappointed. And that tiny, tough girl who strong-armed her way to the ceiling is not someone who looks like she'd be bummed about missing a cornball square dance.

I'd obviously never taken the time to look hard enough.

"Well," Mouth said.

We all turned. It was the first time he'd spoken all afternoon.

"There's an advantage to holding the dance after wrestling practice."

"What's that?" Aleck asked encouragingly.

"It already smells like a barn in here!"

While I was happy to see Mouth returning to his jokey self, I wished his recovery hadn't been at Molly's expense. I mean, who'd blame her for getting upset? Her sweat had contributed to the B.O. he was joking about! But Molly totally took me by surprise—again!—by looking directly at Mouth and letting out a huge whoop of laughter.

And that's when I had another brilliant idea. I just had to ask.

And this time, I didn't hesitate.

Chapter Twenty-Three

I didn't leave myself much time to get ready for the dance. But that's okay because Sara was right about my beauty routine being pretty much nonexistent. Tonight it was a notch above nonexistent because I actually took my hair out of its ponytail and tried a half-up/half-down style my sister had shown me. Hope and I knew the Supersquare would go over the top with their matchy-matchy Chic Boutique formalwear, so we decided the Leftovers could wear whatever we wanted. I chose a freshly laundered version of what I usually wear to school: jeans and a vintage Dolly Parton T-shirt. I thought it was hilarious because Dolly is legendarily well-endowed, and I am not.

My mother had read in the newsletter that the theme was "square-dance chic" and "haute couture country." I did not expect her to take this so literally. I would've laughed when I saw my parents, if I weren't so totally horrified.

"NOOOOOOOO!"

"I knew it was too much," Dad said.

"Nonsense!" Mom said. "It's perfect."

"No," I said, pointing to Mom's glittery cowgirl hat.

"No," I said, pointing to Dad's rhinestone bolo tie.

No to the matching fringed vests. No to the color-coordinated neck bandannas. No to enormous BORN IN THE USA belt buckles. NO. NO. NO. And NOPE.

"It's not a costume party! It's not Halloween! Please put on normal parent clothes! PLEEEEEEEEEASE!"

I was literally on my knees, begging at their rainbow-embroidered cowboy boots.

"She's right," Dad said. "I feel ridiculous."

"That's because you look ridiculous!"

My mother shot us both disappointed looks.

"But it's a theme party! They're always so much fun!"

"For the kids!" Dad shot back. "Not the chaperones!"

"I'm not going anywhere with you two dressed like that." I defiantly crossed my arms. "I mean it!"

Did I mean it? Was I willing to let down the Leftovers to selfishly spare myself the humiliation of being seen with my parents in public dressed like rejects from a rhinestone rodeo?

My dad took off his hat and started unbuttoning his vest as he headed upstairs.

"Where are you going?" Mom asked.

"You can stay as you are," Dad said. "But I'm changing into something more *me*."

"More boring," Mom said with a deep sigh.

Less than five minutes later, my dad was back downstairs and dressed like his normal boring self in a dress shirt and khakis. And though my mom hadn't changed a thing about her own outfit, their overall impact as a couple was way less ridiculous than it was before. I could live with it. Besides, Mr. Armbruster's first call was set to begin in ten minutes, so it was far too late for her to change, even if she wanted to.

I was the last of the Leftovers to get there. Hope, Basketball Mike, the Scouts, Aleck, Mouth, and Molly were all waiting for me at the entrance to the gym.

"I thought you bailed on me!" Hope said. "On us!"

"Never!" I said. I gestured toward my mother. "We had a bit of a wardrobe crisis."

On cue, Aleck said, "Nice outfit, Mrs. Darling."

"Why, thank you!" Mom looked at me pointedly. "See? At least someone appreciates my efforts!"

"Come on," Molly said, simultaneously pushing Aleck and pulling Mouth through the doors. "We don't want to be late!"

And yet, despite our rush, we all stopped dead when we got inside. The gym had been transformed into a spectacularly bedazzled farmstead.

"Wow!" my dad said, taking it all in. "This is something else!"

"See that silver cow with the bow tie?" I asked.

"Holy cow!" Dad laughed. "How could I miss it?"

"I made that," I bragged.

"You did?"

I would've pointed out all the hard work Aleck and Mouth had put into constructing the gorgeous, glittering barnyard, but there wasn't time, because the Leftovers had a Hoedown Showdown to win.

No surprise, the Supersquare took up the most visible spot, right in the middle of the dance floor. The eight of us held our heads high as we passed them. Mouth was right next to me, so I couldn't help but notice when his bottom lip began to quiver. Molly must have seen it, too, because she sped up to walk beside him, and took his hand in a show of support.

"Omigod! The losers have arrived!"

I didn't want to give them the satisfaction of checking them out. But I couldn't stop myself. The boys—Burke and Scotty included—looked deceptively mature in matching dark suits. I was stunned to see Manda, Sara, Dori, and

Bridget all wearing the controversial black-and-white Chic Boutique dress! By some trick of fashion magic, the same strapless fit-and-flare style complemented each of their very different body types. The girls looked lovelier than I'd ever seen them, which I hated to admit—even to myself— because their actions had been so *un*lovely lately.

Leave it to Hope to be the better person I wanted to be.

"You all look beautiful," Hope said. "Good luck."

"Omigod."

"Um."

"Like…"

"Thanks?"

The girls were obviously flustered by Hope's unexpected gesture of goodwill.

"Works every time," she said just loud enough for me to hear.

"What does?"

She smiled wickedly. "Crushing them with kindness."

So the Leftovers took our spot in the way, way back corner of the gym. We got ourselves into position, and okay, I guess this is when I should mention how Aleck became my partner. It's not an exciting story, really, not the kind that another type of girl could retell and review and retell and review with all her friends over and over and over again. Here it is:

Mouth and Molly had partnered up, leaving me with Aleck.

So I'd said, "Um. I guess we're partners."

And he'd said, "I guess so."

And that was it.

Only that wasn't it at all. It was only just beginning. And I know this is the part when I'm supposed to tell you every last detail about the Hoedown Showdown. But I can't. And not because I don't want to, but because I'm still not quite sure what happened. But I'll do my best.

It started out innocently enough. Mr. Armbruster—wearing a one-hundred-gallon cowboy hat my mom must have totally envied—started us off easy with songs and patterns we'd learned in gym class. Because the Leftovers had never practiced together as a group, we figured we'd need a few warm-up dances to get used to one another.

A plucky banjo launched into a familiar number called "Chicken in the Frying Pan."

"Yeehaw!" yelped Aleck. "I love this one!"

"Me too!" said Basketball Mike.

"It's good," Mouth agreed.

"But 'Jersey Devil Went Down to Pineville' is better, right?" said Molly.

"I agree!" Hope chimed in.

"Us too!" added the Scouts.

Aleck's hand never got gross and sweaty like Scotty's. Maybe that's why I was actually enjoying myself. For real. We all were. Honestly, we didn't need a warm-up. We were so in sync, right from the beginning, moving effortlessly from one pattern into the next. I imagine if you had watched us from above, like from the top of Molly's rope, the eight of us would've resembled the shape-shifting gems at the bottom of a kaleidoscope.

Song after song, call after call, we paid no mind to the Supersquare or anyone else. All around us, the judges Mr. Armbruster had brought in from the International Square Dance Association eliminated the clumsier squares one by one. Before long, there were way more kids clapping in time from the sidelines than on the actual dance floor.

Mr. Armbruster made a big announcement at the end of a song called "Swing, Swang, Swung Yer Partner."

"We're down to our top three squares!"

For the first time since the music began, the Leftovers took notice of what was left of our competition. It was down to us, a square of 8th-Grade Hots in matching red-white-and-blue overalls, and—of course—the Supersquare. The competition had definitely taken a toll on them. At some point, the boys had removed their jackets and ties, revealing deep rings of armpit sweat. The girls had fared even worse. Dori's updo had fallen apart. Manda's mascara was smudged up to her eyebrows, and her lipstick was smeared down to her chin. Sara's self-tanner had stained orange streaks on the white bodice of her dress. Only Bridget would've looked as pretty as ever—if she weren't scowling at Burke.

In our T-shirts and jeans and official Scout uniforms, the Leftovers looked like we always do—only happier.

"It's time for the Hoedown Showdown!" announced Mr. Armbruster. "'Jersey Devil Went Down to Pineville'!"

The final dance began with a sizzling fiddle riff. Hope and I met in the center of the square and coached each other with our eyes.

IT'S NOW OR NEVER.

TIME TO FLY THE COOP.

And so we did.

The Leftovers were quick to notice that Hope and I had stopped following Mr. Armbruster's calls and were going freestyle with our moves. I mean, how could you not notice the two of us swiveling our hips and waving our arms and shaking our rumps to the beat of the washtub bass?

The Leftovers froze with panic.

Except Aleck. If it weren't for Aleck, it all would have ended right there.

But it didn't.

Because Aleck intuitively jumped in the center and shouted, "We're squiggle dancing!"

He was right. We were *square dancing with wiggle room for creative interpretation*, as he'd put it. And it was exactly what Bethany had instructed us to do. Within seconds, the rest of the Leftovers caught on and were squiggle dancing right along with us. It was an awesome display of spontaneous synchronization! And synchronized spontaneity! What made sense to us must have looked like chaos to everyone else. I can only imagine the reactions coming from Sara's square.

"OMIGOD! What are they doing?"

"Puh-leeze! Who cares? We're winning!"

"It's like they're messing up on purpose!"

I don't know if they actually said these things, because I didn't hear a word Sara, Manda, Dori, or anyone else was saying. I was too in the music, too in the movement, too in the moment. So I totally missed it when Mr. Armbruster fell off his hay bale and shouted, "SWEET JUMPIN' JEHOSHAPHAT! THEY'RE FLYING THE COOP!"

For the duration of a song, I felt one hundred percent free, as if I'd never again be burdened by stressing, obsessing, or second-guessing. And that blissful liberation was the greatest reward of all.

Yes, even better than defeating the Supersquare and being declared the winners of the Hoedown Showdown.

Chapter Twenty-Four

Six out of eight members of the Supersquare shrugged off the loss. But Sara and Manda weren't going down without a fight.

"Omigod! Mr. Armbruster! They cheated!"

"Flying the coop? Puh-leeze. There's no such thing!"

Mr. Armbruster and the International Square Dance Association judges assured them that we did not cheat and that there *is* such a thing. They would not waver in their decision, even after Sara made the usual threats about Daddy's lawyer.

"The decision stands!" Mr. Armbruster took off his cowboy hat and threw it into the air. "These are our champions!"

And the eight of us had just enough time for a group

WHOOP! before my parents came rushing at me with eyes bigger than their belt buckles.

"Jessie! I never knew you had it in you!" Mom marveled.

"Had what in me?" I asked.

"Whatever it was we just saw!" Dad joked.

Added bonus to being in the moment? The whole time I was dancing, I didn't worry about how my parents might be embarrassing me. And I was on such a hoedown high, I actually told them so.

"I know I gave you a hard time—" I started.

"See?" Mom interrupted. "I told you it would be fun for all of us!"

My mother is never above an I-told-you-so. NEVER.

"You did," my dad admitted. "You told us so."

And then he patted me on the back to let me know he found Mom's I-told-you-so as irritating as I did.

"I'm happy you came," I admitted when we reached the car. "Because I have no idea how I would've described what happened!"

And for the first time in a long time, all three of us laughed.

Everyone was being picked up by their parents at the same time. It was a sloooooow exit out of the parking lot. There was a lot of noise, so it took a minute before I realized the car next to us was honking rhythmically to get our attention.

Honk! Honk! Honkity-honk!
Honk! Honk! Honkity-honk!
Honk! Honk! Honkity-honk!

Aleck was in the passenger seat of the honking car. He gestured for me to roll down the window.

"I'm really glad you asked me to be your partner!"

Me too, I thought, before quickly taking it back in my brain because I *hadn't* asked him to be my partner. Molly and Mouth had paired up, so it just kind of worked out that way. But I didn't say this or anything else too revealing, because my parents were listening and my mom would ask, like, a bazillion questions about who Aleck is and what exactly I'd meant when I said those two words, and I was already semireading all her questions about the dance itself and just couldn't deal with a whole new interrogation on top of it.

So I just rolled my eyes and half smiled like "Okay. Whatever you say."

And then he shouted something I couldn't quite hear over the rumble of all the idling car engines.

"What?"

"I said," he shouted louder, "I guess you really do miss me when I'm not around!"

THAT'S WHAT I'D THOUGHT HE SAID.

Did this mean Aleck didn't burn the Top Secret Pineville Junior High Crushability Quiz like he said he did?

Or did he read it first, then burn it? Or did he not read it at all and burned it like he said he did and he's just innocently joking around and I'm just totally paranoid because I know I wrote his name for dumb trick question #5 and he doesn't?

But then the traffic opened up, and his car sped off, and I didn't get to any of those questions—not that I would have shouted them out the window with my parents in the front seat. To be honest, I doubt I'll ask Aleck in Woodshop on Monday, either, even if it's my only opportunity to confront him somewhere he can't make a quick escape. Because if there's anything I've learned about stressing, obsessing, and second-guessing, it's this: I'm much better off when I don't try so hard to know everything.

Chapter Twenty-Five

It was an eventful weekend.

Bridget broke up with Burke for being a jerk. Manda tried to make up with Mouth. Mouth and Molly held hands at the movies. Sara shopped everywhere but Chic Boutique. Bridget forgave Burke for being a jerk. Manda re-rebounded with Vinnie. The Scouts earned merit badges in folk dancing. Heath remembered to wear his helmet and taught Aleck a new skateboard maneuver. I wrote a thank-you poem for my sister, and Hope illustrated it with cartoon-chicken versions of us flying the coop.

By the time I walked into homeroom, Pineville Junior High had already turned its collective attention to hotter topics than our victory at the Down-Home Harvest Dance. Only Mr. Armbruster was still enthralled by what he'd seen that night. He couldn't wait to give the whole class his play-by-play color commentary on my winning square's fly-the-coop coup.

"I tell you, I haven't seen anything like that since the Northeastern Square Dance Semifinals in 1982."

He certainly would have gone on for the next ten minutes if he hadn't been interrupted by the buzz of the intercom.

"Mr. Armbruster, please send Jessica Darling to Principal Masters's office immediately."

Everyone "ooh-OOH-oohed" on cue because it's mandatory to do so whenever anyone gets called to the principal's office, especially when it's somebody unexpected like me. Only Sara looked unsurprised. She counted off my offenses on her fingers.

"Number one: You cheated. Number two: Your square engaged in inappropriate body contact. And number three: Your parents neglected their duties as chaperones. It's time for justice."

I should have known Sara would get the administration involved. We hadn't cheated. Mr. Armbruster would back me up on that for sure. But on the way to the office, I considered the other charges and was less certain of my innocence. Had we engaged in inappropriate body contact? Would my parents get in trouble for not stopping it?

I didn't have any time to collect my thoughts. Mr. Masters was ready and waiting for me upon my arrival at his office.

"Come in, Jessica," he said brusquely. "Let's talk."

He was smiling, but in a distracted way. I felt my mouth smile back at him with similar insincerity. He took a seat behind his desk, and I took one in front. A PJHS mug was filled to the brim with milky coffee. An untouched powdered doughnut waited on his mouse pad.

"A student is joining the seventh-grade Gifted and Talented classes. We've chosen you to be a goodwill ambassador for the school."

Wow. He wasn't wasting a single second.

"What do you think of that?"

I was thinking he was rushing me through this ambassadorship so he could get going on that coffee and doughnut. He didn't wait for an answer.

"Great! You'll help our new addition adjust to life here at Pineville Junior High."

He was already standing up to show me out.

"But new kids transfer into our school all the time," I said, still sitting. "None of them have been assigned goodwill ambassadors."

He slowly sat back down again. His eyes flickered toward the doughnut, then regained focus.

"This student is special. Actually, *extraordinary* is a better word for it. She's brilliant. A genius. Any school would be lucky to have her, and to think her family chose Pineville Junior High over other educational opportunities is quite an honor."

Extraordinary? Brilliant? Genius?

I gulped.

Mr. Masters consulted a folder with my name on it. You know how we're always warned that bad behavior will be put on our "permanent record"? Until then, I'd thought that was just a made-up threat to keep us in line. But he actually had my "permanent record" in his hands!

"You have top grades, no disciplinary problems..."

He flipped through the pages. There were a lot of pages. It seemed like too many pages for a twelve-year-old seventh grader with top grades and no disciplinary problems. What filled so many pages?

"You show promise as an athlete," Mr. Masters continued. "And you demonstrated school spirit as the cochair of the Down-Home Harvest Dance and during your brief but memorable turn as the Pineville Junior High mascot."

Wait. What? Whoa.

How had Mighty the Seagull gotten on my permanent record? It was supposed to be a secret! WORST-KEPT SECRET OF ALL TIME.

I would've laughed out loud if I weren't so freaked out by whatever else there could be about me in that folder. Who knew what I'd learn about myself if I could only get a look? But Mr. Masters shut it before I could even think of sneaking a peek.

"In short," he said as he ushered me out of his office, "you're the best Pineville Junior High has to offer."

I know he meant it as a compliment, but for some reason it didn't feel like one. I turned around to thanks-but-no-thanks him for the opportunity, but my principal's mustache was already dusted with powdered sugar. Our conversation was over.

I left our meeting with mixed emotions. On the upside: I was the best our school had to offer. On the downside: Our school's best was hardly good enough for an extraor-dinary, brilliant genius.

These conflicted feelings churned inside my belly, so I took a detour to the girls' bathroom to splash cold water on my face. I'd heard the expression *green with envy*, of course. But I'd never known it could be taken literally until I looked up from the sink and saw myself in the bathroom mirror. I was already sick with jealousy about a person I'd never met.

I'm the Smart One. Everyone says so.

Who will I be if the new girl is smarter than me?

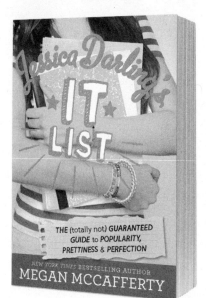